C000135656

The Endeavours of Sherlock Holmes

By

Mark Wardecker

First edition published in 2022
© Copyright 2022
Mark Wardecker

The right of Mark Wardecker to be identified as the author of this work has been asserted by him in accordance with the Copyright, Designs and Patents Act 1998.

All rights reserved. No reproduction, copy or transmission of this publication may be made without express prior written permission. No paragraph of this publication may be reproduced, copied or transmitted except with express prior written permission or in accordance with the provisions of the Copyright Act 1956 (as amended). Any person who commits any unauthorised act in relation to this publication may be liable to criminal prosecution and civil claims for damage.

All characters appearing in this work are fictitious. Any resemblance to real persons, living or dead, is purely coincidental. The opinions expressed herein are those of the author and not of MX Publishing.

Hardcover ISBN 978-1-80424-052-6
Paperback ISBN 978-1-80424-053-3
ePub ISBN 978-1-80424-054-0
PDF ISBN 978-1-80424-055-7

Published by MX Publishing
335 Princess Park Manor, Royal Drive,
London, N11 3GX
www.mxpublishing.co.uk

Cover design by Brian Belanger

**For William Laughlin
(1964-2004)**

*And with thanks to Chris Fowler and David
Marcum.*

Contents

The Adventure of the Docklands Apparition

When trying to select which of my friend, Sherlock Holmes', cases to lay before the public, I have often had to take consistency into account. For it was not unusual, given the many puzzles and problems with which he was presented, that a client's story might seem to contain those elements of the unique and even grotesque that Holmes found so gratifying, only for the case to later evaporate into the banal and the commonplace. Often, the most absorbing investigations began humbly, with a detail that seemed just slightly awry, such as a discarded photograph of a lady found lying upon the ground. And not since our encounter with the notorious Irene Adler had a photograph of a beautiful woman posed such a threat to a nation's stability as the one in the case I am about to relate.

It was on a gloomy, rainy day in the spring of 1896, just after Holmes and I had finished lunch, when Mrs Hudson entered our sitting room to announce Mr August Pierpont, a tall and sturdy man with graying sideburns and moustache.

"I am sorry to interrupt your meal, Mr Holmes and Dr Watson. If you like, I can return later, but circumstances have become unnerving enough that I felt I should waste no time in seeing you."

As Holmes regarded the man's flushed countenance and agitated respiration, he smiled slightly and replied, "Of course, Mr Pierpont, I would be happy to hear about these circumstances which have so unnerved you. Please, have a seat by the fire and tell us your story from the beginning. Watson,

1

please pour our guest some brandy to calm him, and Mrs Hudson, those dishes can wait. Please make yourself scarce." Holmes took a seat by the fire and relit his pipe as he waited for our indignant landlady to depart and for our guest to sit down.

"Now, Mr Pierpont, please proceed. I realise that you will need to be getting back to the bank soon."

"But, Mr Holmes, how could you know?"

"It is simplicity itself. Your frock coat and pants are of the very best black broadcloth, yet they have become somewhat shiny in the back, suggesting a job that requires you to remain sedentary for long periods. The slight stoop in your shoulders also marks you as a man who spends most of his time hunched over his desk. The pink corner of the *Financial Times* in your inner pocket suggests that you have something to do with finance, and the traces on the fingers and thumb of your right hand of that rosin that is frequently used by people who spend a great deal of their time counting money is also suggestive. Finally, that small, gold ornament depending from your fob with the initials, "IBE", engraved upon it is conclusive: you are employed by the Imperial Bank of England on Lombard Street. As I noted before, you are too well dressed to be a clerk, but I know you are not the director or branch manager of that particular establishment. I'd venture, though, that you are in a position of some authority."

"I'm an accounts manager for the Imperial Bank. That is uncanny, Mr Holmes!"

"Please, state your case," replied Holmes as he leaned back into his armchair and assumed the weary, heavy-lidded expression which veiled his keen and eager nature.

"Well, Mr Holmes, it may be as nothing, but three days ago an odd series of seeming coincidences began to unfold before me. I'm a bachelor and own a small house in Christopher Street, Finsbury. As I was leaving for work Monday morning, I noticed what appeared to be a piece of litter lying on the stoop outside my front door. When I attempted to sweep it aside with my foot, it clung there stubbornly, so I knelt to pick it up. Mr Holmes, it was a photograph of a woman."

Fishing in one of his waistcoat pockets, Pierpont retrieved a small photograph of the most striking women I had ever seen. Raven-black hair framed a delicately and perfectly proportioned face of almost porcelain complexion, and there was an intensity in her dark eyes that gave the photograph an extraordinarily lifelike quality.

"The back of the picture is still slightly tacky with adhesive," observed Holmes. "May I keep this?"

"Of course. I only kept it on the off chance that I might bump into its subject in the neighbourhood and return it." As he said this, a flush once again returned to his countenance.

"You do not know the subject?"

"I'd never seen her before then, Mr Holmes. But on my way to work that morning, just as I was entering the bank, I saw her standing just outside a jeweller's, five doors down. I could not help but stare, and as I stood there trying to determine if it was, in fact, the same woman, she turned and seemed to recognize me. She took a step toward me, but I then lost sight of her as a passing throng of young clerks passed by. I stood there, like a fool, for some time but was unable to spot her again."

"So you're unsure that it was the same woman?"

3

"I was, Mr Holmes, but the thing that is so extraordinary is that I've seen her several times since. As you have noted, I don't have much opportunity to stretch my legs at the bank, and I try to walk as much as possible. However, on Monday evening, I worked rather late and decided to take a cab home. But just as I was putting the key in the front door of my house, I saw her again. She was walking toward me, and I had just caught sight of her before she turned into an alley three houses down from my house. I could hardly believe my eyes and immediately turned to follow her, but when I turned into the alley, there was no sign of her. Yesterday, I saw her again, both as I was arriving at and departing from work, and again, she vanished as suddenly as she appeared."

"Did she appear near the jeweller's yesterday, as well?"

"Yes, in that vicinity. I was relating the events to two of the clerks at work, and one of them joked that it sounded like a case for Sherlock Holmes.

"For lunch, I decided to take advantage of the break in the rain and walk to the George and Vulture. As I turned into Birchin Lane, there she was again! She was on the opposite side of the street and walking in the opposite direction. It did not look as though she had seen me, so I followed her, sticking to the opposite side of the road. We made our way almost as far south as Cannon Street before an omnibus passed between us, and I lost sight of her."

"Could you tell from where she'd come?" asked Holmes.

"No, she seems to appear and vanish like a ghost. I could stand no more and immediately resolved to hail a cab and, all jesting aside, consult you."

"Your story contains elements that intrigue me, Mr Pierpont, but I'm afraid that there is not yet a sufficient amount of data with which to work. I do promise to assist you, if necessary, in this matter and will ask you to please leave me your card and home address. Do not hesitate to contact me if anything else of significance happens. Watson will see you to the door."

With that, I led our guest back out and reassured him as he donned his hat and coat that Holmes would do everything in his power to help and that he should not worry about imposing upon us in the future. When I returned to our sitting room, Holmes was still sitting with his feet upon the fireplace fender, puffing away at his oily, black clay pipe.

"It is remarkable the lengths to which an old bachelor will go having caught sight of a pretty face," I remarked.

"A phenomenon with which you are no doubt familiar," retorted Holmes, smiling.

"Well, to be fair, if her photograph does her any justice at all, I probably would not object to walking after her in the rain, either."

"Then you shall have your chance. I have a small matter to attend to in the morning. I was hoping you would follow Mr Pierpont to work tomorrow morning and report back to me everything that you see," said Holmes as he stood and handed Pierpont's card to me.

I assured Holmes that he could rely upon me, and next morning found me standing half a block from the banker's neat, three-story home in Christopher Street. It had stopped raining but a cold, damp fog had settled heavily upon The City, and when I saw Pierpont hail a cab, I immediately did the same, taking care not to be seen by him. On the way from his front door to the hansom, I noticed no change in his behaviour, and we travelled slowly but without incident to Lombard Street. As he alighted from the cab, however, Pierpont turned dramatically and stared intently to his right. I quickly left my cab and tried to follow his gaze but could only see hoards of clerks, businessmen, and workmen all rushing about their customary early morning business in The City. Pierpont began to look rather wild and rushed down the street. Trying to be discreet, I was at a disadvantage as I followed him, but I was certain that, if our mysterious lady were somewhere in Lombard Street, I would surely have seen her. After having gotten about halfway down the block, I turned quickly into a tobacco shop as Pierpont returned dejectedly to the bank. Once he was out of sight, I continued to reconnoitre, but I never did glimpse the black-haired woman from the photograph.

I had just finished lunch when Holmes returned to Baker Street, and I related to him all that had occurred that morning.

"I am sorry I don't have more for you, Holmes."

"Not at all. Your professional opinion may be of value here. Did Pierpont seem . . . healthy to you . . . *compos mentis*?"

"Actually, Holmes when I saw the change in his features as he got out of the cab, I did become concerned. But of course, under the circumstances, there is no way to be certain about the state of his mind."

"No, but it is, at least, another possibility. But what is this?"

A frantic banging at the front door had begun, and soon, above Mrs Hudson's protestations, I could hear rapid footsteps on the stairs. Looking even more worryingly frantic than before, Mr Pierpont burst into our quarters.

"Mr Holmes, I saw her again! And she led me straight to a murder!"

"A murder? Mr Pierpont, this is really most grat . . . fascinating. Please, take off your coat and have a seat. Have you informed the police?"

After helping the banker out of his coat and pouring a drink, we sat down to hear his story.

"I have told Inspector Lestrade, who is the detective in charge. He told me he would wait for you at the scene of the crime."

"Then we must not keep him waiting. Please, from the beginning."

"Since I was unable to go yesterday, I thought I would walk to the George and Vulture for lunch today. Again, as I turned the corner into Birchin Lane, I saw the woman from the photograph on the other side of the street, heading in the opposite direction. This time, given the fog, I resolved to take no chances. I darted across the street, and after miraculously emerging in one piece onto the other side, I commenced to follow her. I was bolder this time, but she did not turn around as we headed south, past Cannon Street and, eventually, past

Upper Thames Street. However, I was afraid she did spy me as she pivoted on her heel and quickly turned into a side street. Afraid of losing her, I quickened my pace and managed to catch up again before she turned into another, even narrower alley. It seemed remarkable that she wouldn't have spotted me as we wove through these tiny, dirty thoroughfares. Though I was unfamiliar with the neighbourhood, I could tell we were still bearing south in an extremely roundabout way. And as crumbling tenements gave way to even seedier pubs and sooty warehouses, I could also tell we were getting very close to the Thames. I determined finally to call out to her, because I was truly concerned for her safety as I saw sailors, dockworkers, and assorted riffraff leering at her out of the fog. But just as I opened my mouth to yell, we suddenly emerged onto the docks, the Christopher Docks, to be precise and as I later learned.

"She never said a word, Mr Holmes, but abruptly stopped and stepped to one side, looking toward two figures on the dock who were barely visible in the dense riverside fog. I was unprepared to stop and came within less than ten feet of the two men before halting. To my surprise, one of them was another accounts manager from my bank, a Mr Lewis Owen. He was on his knees and seemed to be unconscious. The other man, who was unknown to me, had a hold of Owen from under his arms, a truncheon still gripped in his right hand. I called Owens' name, barely realising what I was doing, but it was too late. The ruffian had already swung him around and pushed him into the river. The murderous brute then turned upon me, brandishing the truncheon, and I'm ashamed to say, I turned and ran faster than I've ever run.

"I'd gotten no further than two blocks from the docks before seeing a constable and calling for help. My pursuer, however, had abandoned the chase and had disappeared back into the fog. The constable and I rushed back to the dock to help poor Lewis, but all we saw of him, upon returning, was his top hat floating the water. I told him my story and repeated it to Inspector Lestrade when he arrived on the scene."

"And what did our friend, Lestrade, make of the affair?"

"He seemed to think it was merely a mugging that had gone too far."

"And his thoughts on the woman?"

"He appeared uninterested."

"Typical. I don't suppose you saw what happened to her?"

"No, Mr Holmes, She was gone when I turned to run."

"And the assailant's appearance?"

"He was about my height in rough brown tweed and a misshapen brown bowler. His face, what I could make out, was clean-shaven. He was a little remarkable looking in that his mouth was rather long, almost reptilian looking, and he had either no or very thin eyebrows."

"This is really most interesting," remarked Holmes with that keen look in his eyes that always preceded the hunt.

"I don't know. What if I have been beset by a spirit from the other plane, sent as a harbinger of doom and disaster? Dear God! What if I should continue seeing her?"

"Please restrain yourself, Mr Pierpont. That you were being led somewhere is certain, but we must confine ourselves to physical entities of a far more commonplace type. How well did you know the victim?"

"Not very. He began working at the bank about five months ago, replacing Peters when he left unexpectedly. I know that he did good work, but he kept mostly to himself. He never mentioned a family or anything about his social life."

"Please think. Is there anything to connect you with Owen?

"I'm sorry, but I can think of nothing. We worked in the same bank but never exchanged anything more than the most casual of greetings."

"Do you know if he was friends with any of the other employees?"

"Not that I'm aware of. He came to the bank promptly every morning and departed by himself in the evening."

"Alright, Mr Pierpont. Are you returning to the bank now? Good. Watson and I need to meet with Lestrade while there is still a chance his men have not entirely obliterated every scrap of evidence from the scene. We will stop by the bank afterwards."

Holmes and I took a cab to the Christopher Docks, and the ride was made interminably long by both the fog and by Holmes having fallen into one of his fits of reticence. Upon disembarking from the cab, once we had arrived at our destination, a smile returned to his face as he addressed our old comrade, and occasional rival, Inspector Lestrade.

"Greetings, Lestrade! I hear you have met one of my clients."

The cold, dirty fog was even denser here by the river, and it really did feel like we were on a different plane, with the shades of policemen, sailors, and stevedores hovering around us. Lestrade peered at us through the mist.

"It seems you are one step ahead of us this time, Mr Holmes. But never you worry. We'll close the gap before long."

"I have every faith."

"So, have you learned anything relevant from your client?"

"To be honest, I sent him on his way yesterday, because there seemed too little to go on. All that had happened were his continual encounters with the woman in this photograph," said Holmes, handing the picture to Lestrade. "You may keep that."

"Thank you, Holmes. He told us about his series of run-ins with the lady. At first, I thought them insignificant, but now I'm not so sure."

"What's made you change your mind?"

"It seemed, at first, like a routine mugging in a dangerous area, but then, a few moments ago, when he overheard me mention that the poor fellow worked for the Imperial Bank, one of the other detectives mentioned that that bank's director is at present being done for embezzlement."

"You don't say."

"Now I'm wondering if Owen were somehow involved in this mess?"

"You know, Holmes," I interjected, "you said something earlier about Pierpont being led here. What if the woman was trying to lead him here to prevent this from happening?"

"It's a leap. Pierpont isn't the first person to whom I would turn for protection, but leaps of the imagination are crucial in situations like these. Have your men found the body?"

"No, just Owen's hat floating in the river. I've already requested some boats to drag for him, but it will probably be some time before they get here, given the weather."

"I don't suppose there were any witnesses?"

"Here? The lads are talking to people, but I wouldn't hold my breath."

"May I take a look?"

"By all means," replied Lestrade and handed Holmes a bull's-eye lantern, for despite its being mid-afternoon, it was becoming quite dark.

After closely examining the bricks of the docks for several minutes, Holmes returned the lantern.

"Do you have anything to add, Holmes?" asked Lestrade.

"Only that the ground corroborates Pierpont's account, nothing more than we already know. There is a fine layer of mud that has been disturbed which could be indicative of a struggle, but there is no way of making out any prints. There are also some clothing threads that match his description of the subject. If you find the body or get anything out of the director, please let me know."

"And where are you headed?"

"To the bank for now. Tomorrow, I shall try to learn more of Mr Lewis Owen. I'll let you know if I find anything of interest."

We returned to our awaiting cab and proceeded north to Lombard Street and the Imperial Bank. When we arrived a short time later, the disruption caused by the director's arrest was still very much in evidence as both staff and patrons milled nervously about the large, marble lobby and desperate sounding clerks attempted to placate frightened sounding customers. Evidently, the arrest had already reached the newspapers. We entered a doorway to the left and walked down a narrow, wainscoted hallway to Pierpont's office. As we reached his door, he was just ushering out a sceptical looking older man, asserting repeatedly that the client's investments were perfectly safe. He seemed glad of any distraction and invited us in. Before entering, Holmes stopped to examine a photograph that hung on the wall.

"It is a picture from our last annual Christmas party," offered Pierpont.

"Is Owen in it?"

"Why, yes, he is. Right . . . here."

"May I borrow it?"

Pierpont looked at Holmes dubiously and then shrugged.

"I don't suppose, at present, that anyone will miss it," he said, sighing.

After sitting down in some plush, leather armchairs before Pierpont's large, mahogany desk, Holmes asked the banker if he had been able to discover anything more about his murdered coworker.

"I'm sorry, Mr Holmes, but in all of today's chaos, I haven't had time to talk to anyone about him. As soon as things settle down, I'll try to learn more."

"That is perfectly understandable given the circumstances. There is one point on which you can probably enlighten me, however. Would Owen have been in a position to discover your director's embezzling?"

"Well, Mr Holmes, without yet knowing the exact circumstances, it would be hard to say. Obviously, he, and I for that matter, have access to the records of every account, including those of the director. If funds were being misappropriated in such a way that it would be discoverable from those records, then he could conceivably have uncovered what was going on. I must say, however, that I would hope a bank's director, even a crooked one, would be a little more clever."

"Thank you. If you find out more, please let us know. I shall be in touch."

As Holmes and I made our way back through the crowd in the echoing lobby, I attempted to sound him out.

"Not very much to go on, is it?"

"I shall certainly need more data. It is a capital mistake to theorise without data, and I doubt we shall be able to gather more until tomorrow. What do you say to dinner at Simpson's?"

That was as much about the case as I was able to get out of Holmes that evening, and after dinner, during which Holmes spoke at length about Vergil's *Georgics* and the light that work shed upon the qualities of bees, we returned to Baker Street. I turned in early and awoke shortly after dawn but found that Holmes had already departed. I heard nothing from that entire day until a telegram arrived in the early evening:

"Come to the Diogenes Club at 6:30 if convenient. If inconvenient, come all the same."

Fortunately, I was available and so not overly annoyed at Holmes' summons. I arrived at that curious club where members are forbidden to speak or to take the least notice of each other. I was then ushered by a servant into the Stranger's Room, the only room in which guests and conversation were permitted. Holmes had already arrived and stood to greet me. Another man began to laboriously lift himself from his chair, and I recognized him even before he had turned around to greet me. Mycroft Holmes, Sherlock Holmes' older brother, was of considerably greater girth than his sibling, but he possessed the same keen, steel-gray eyes as his brother. According to Holmes, Mycroft's deductive and reasoning powers exceeded his own, and the specialism he provided his employer, the British government, was no less than "omniscience". Mycroft was also a founding member of this peculiar club and, when not at his lodgings in Pall Mall, could invariably either be found here or in Whitehall. After we had all exchanged greetings, we sat down, and Holmes began to address us.

"Your timing is excellent, Watson. I was just recounting the events of the past few days to brother Mycroft and just arrived at my breakthrough today at Somerset House. That is where I spent the entire day, going through the records of several of the government offices that are housed there. I was hoping there would be something—a will, an insurance policy, anything—that might shed some light on our missing banker."

"But Holmes, Owen isn't really missing. He's no doubt lying at the bottom of the Thames," I argued.

"No, Watson," he said smiling, "even when we were at the docks yesterday, I had serious doubts that a murder had actually been committed. The whole scenario seemed too obviously staged. The appearance of the photograph and the woman, the way she contrived to get Pierpont to follow her, it reminded me of other such cases. You noticed yourself yesterday that Pierpont was being led. Why? Was he being led *away from* The City so that a crime could be perpetrated, just as Hall Pycroft was led *away from* Mawson & Williams or Jabez Wilson was led away from his pawnshop in the affair of the red-headed men? Or was it to lead him *to* somewhere, possibly to witness a crime, like John Scott Eccles when he visited Wisteria Lodge? The elaborate tableau at the scene of the crime and commitment of Owen to his part suggested the latter. Very few men would be willing to take a swim in the Thames at this time of year. Also, aside from the ongoing fraud of the director, who was already in the process of being apprehended, there was no evidence of any other crime.

"But there was another detail, one of those trivialities which often proves infinitely important, that kept nagging at me as I leafed through page after page of records."

"That Peters had left unexpectedly?" queried Mycroft.

"Precisely! That Peters, the employee whom Owen had succeeded, had left the bank unexpectedly. I have often expounded upon the importance of imagination to detection, and it was as I was wading through that paperwork and thinking about Peters, that a real possibility began to emerge. What if Peters was coerced or bribed into leaving so that Owen could take his place? It would just be possible if the timing was right, if a word was spoken in the right ear, if there was a director present who was already compromised. This is all simple enough. But why had Owen been planted? What could he have been after? If investigators had been closely watching the bank and building a case against the director, it would have been difficult for Owen to have stolen any money, and recent events seem to indicate a greater sophistication. As I opened yet another manila folder, I had an epiphany. What if it wasn't the actual money or even individual transactions, but about this aggregation of their surrogates, the records and ledgers themselves? One could learn a great deal about people from their financial records: their whereabouts, their travels, their contacts, employers, associations. A criminal or espionage organisation could do much with such information. At the moment, I know of no such criminal enterprise that would be up to such a scheme, not since Moriarty fell to his death at the Reichenbach Falls. But Mycroft, I was wondering if perhaps your people had any dealings with the Imperial Bank?"

"Oh, Sherlock, this time you have outdone yourself. Obviously, this is not to leave this room without my consent, but we do have . . . agents that could possibly be tracked, given this scenario you have constructed. And Adolph Meyer, a particularly slippery German agent, matches Pierpont's description of the eyebrowless, long-mouthed assailant and is known to be in London. I shall see if I can discover his exact whereabouts."

"Excellent. I have already begun a search for Owen and will contact you tomorrow to inform you of its progress."

As we emerged from the Diogenes Club and made our way back into the evening's fog, though it was as yet unknown to me, Holmes' search was already proceeding, as countless urchins, the neglected children of London, crept from alley to alley and from rooftop to rooftop in the murky, gas-lit gloom, in search of the banker, Owen. Holmes had provided Wiggins, the leader of this ragtag legion, which Holmes had dubbed the "Baker Street Irregulars", with the photograph he had borrowed from the bank and offered a reward to the boy that could find Owen first.

While this unseen manhunt continued, Holmes and I returned to Baker Street so that he could root through the agony columns of recent newspapers in search of some communications between the spies. Though Holmes had frequently been rewarded in the past by such sources, he was destined to be frustrated that night. In the early hours of the morning, he must have given up, for I heard from my chamber the discordant tones of his violin below.

By morning, the fog of acrid tobacco smoke in our sitting room rivalled that of the city without. Refusing breakfast, Holmes paced nervously and continued to consume pipe after pipe of shag. Finally, at a little after ten o'clock, a district messenger arrived with word from Mycroft. Much to Holmes' annoyance, he unfortunately had been unable to track down Meyer's whereabouts. But just as the young messenger opened the door to leave the house, a raggedly dressed and dirty adolescent squeezed past him and bounded up the stairs to pound rapidly on our door.

"Ah, Wiggins! I see that for once you have followed my instructions to leave the rest of the lads outside," said Holmes, as he opened the door. "We don't want to upset Mrs Hudson. Now, quickly, have you run our prey to ground?"

"Stinson saw him on his way back to his flat after lunch. He lives at 110 Vine Street in Aldgate, flat number two. He only just told me about it, so Owen should still be there. Stinson posted Buckley to stand watch, just in case, though."

"Excellent, Wiggins! Please give this and my thanks to Stinson and take this for yourself. Also, please go and take this note to Inspector Lestrade at Scotland Yard."

When he had finished writing, he handed the note to Wiggins who bounded back down the stairs with it. At Holmes' suggestion, I retrieved my service revolver and we made our way by cab without delay to Aldgate. We stopped just around the corner from Vine Street and walked to a nearby pub to await Lestrade. We didn't have long to wait, and within half an hour, we had brought Lestrade up to speed over a pint. Having agreed upon a course of action, we departed the pub and walked around the corner into Vine Street. Number 110 was a small, but nondescript house in the centre of the block. In the entrance hall, a small, greasy-haired boy was playing cards, but on seeing Holmes, he gathered up the deck and approached us.

"He's still there, Mr Holmes."

"Thank you, Buckley. If you could do just one more thing for me, there's a shilling in it for you. My friends and I are going to quietly go upstairs and stand by the door of number two. Once we are in position, I want you to come upstairs, bang on the door of the flat, and announce that you have a message

19

for a Mr Owen from a Mr Pierpont. Here, take this in case he can see you from within," said Holmes as he handed the eager boy a blank piece of paper and his shilling.

We made our way silently up the stairs. The apartment was to our left on the second floor, and Holmes moved to the left of the door, while Lestrade and I stood to the right with our revolvers drawn. We were no sooner in place than we heard Buckley come bounding up the stairs. He ran over and stopped before the door.

"Delivery! I have a message for a Mr Owen!" he cried as he knocked on the door. A muffled voice responded from within.

"What? You must be mistaken . . . There's no one here by that name."

"It says it's for Mr Owen of number two from a Mr Pierpont!"

"But that's not . . ."

Suddenly, there was the sound of a bolt being drawn, and the door cautiously opened. Behind it was the man I had seen identified in the photograph at the bank, Mr Lester Owen. The guns Lestrade and I pointed at him were the first things he saw, and he froze as Holmes stepped into the open.

"Hello, Mr Owen. I am Sherlock Holmes, and these are my friends and colleagues, Dr Watson and Inspector Lestrade. Please be so good as to let us in and keep your hands where we can see them."

Owen backed nervously into the one-room flat and took a seat upon the bed as Holmes motioned for him to do. The suitcase that lay open upon it indicated what he had been doing before our arrival.

"Watson, please keep him covered," Holmes requested as Lestrade cuffed Owen's hands together.

"Now, Mr Owen, we can talk, and indeed, it will do you no good to keep silent. We know about your information gathering at the bank, we know about your passing this information on to the German spy, Adolph Meyer, and we know about your attempt to fake your own death so that you could escape punishment for your treason and perhaps go on to repeat it at another establishment."

"Wait! Treason? I'm not sure how, but you seem to know even more of this matter than I."

"Your contact was a known German agent," interjected Lestrade. "And I'm sure you know the penalty for treason."

"If you can explain to us, it might not go as heavily with you," resumed Holmes.

"But what you say can be used against you," added Lestrade.

"I understand, but truly I am no traitor. He called himself Lang, and I didn't know he was a spy . . . or even German, for that matter. He said he only wanted some occasional information—to find out if an account existed for a particular person, if certain transactions were occurring in certain cities, if certain people were conducting business. He wouldn't tell me why, but he offered me enough money that I hardly cared. Of course, I knew it was unethical, but we never stole anything or tampered with any records. Although, now that you have made this accusation, I can see how such information could have been used. But I swear that, at the time, I didn't know!"

"If you are really still at all loyal to your country, I may be able to furnish you with a chance to prove it. But first, what happened to Peters, the man you replaced at the bank?"

"I was going through a rough patch, having just gotten the sack from a position at an insurance company that was about to go under, when I met Lang at Nicholson's Pub. As we spoke, he became more familiar with me and said a position was about to open at the Imperial Bank. He said that if I was to apply, he was sure they would find me to be the right man for the job. He winked and promised to make a considerable investment in me in order to insure it. I knew it wasn't all above board, but I would've grasped at anything in my sorry state."

"Why choose such an elaborate method of disappearing?"

"Lang, or Meyer, was one of those types who thought himself clever. He said he had concocted an ingenious way for me to disappear so that I might be able to work for him elsewhere without a hint of suspicion. He asked me if there was someone at work who knew me and whose testimony would never be questioned. Pierpont seemed perfect. I wasn't exactly thrilled with the prospect of diving into the Thames, but I'm a strong swimmer, and it wasn't as awful as I thought it was going to be. In that dense fog, all I had to do was paddle away a short distance. Meyer then helped to lift me out after pretending to chase Pierpont."

"Who was the woman Pierpont had been following?"

"An associate of Meyer's. I only knew her as Helena, and Meyer had instructed her in advance. Meyer would stand outside the bank and watch for my signal. When I saw Pierpont leaving for lunch, I placed a lamp in my office window with a mirror behind it to increase its illumination. Meyer, upon seeing it, would signal Helena so that she could get a head start. She was to lead Pierpont around through the alleys until we would be ready at the docks, exactly twenty minutes after the signal."

"I think that about answers my questions. Now I will offer you a chance to prevent any further damage resulting from this scheme. Are Meyer and his confederate still in London?"

"I know nothing of her, Mr Holmes, but Meyer said I would be able to reach him until tomorrow if an emergency arose."

"And how would you reach him?"

"There is an unoccupied flat two blocks down the street. It is unfurnished save for a table, a lamp, and a mirror. When I wish to meet with him, I go to the flat and give the same signal that I used at the bank. He then comes here, usually between nine and ten in the evening."

"Very good. Lestrade, Watson and I will go give the signal and notify my brother, Mycroft, that we may yet be able to apprehend Meyer. Meet us back here in an hour with some of your men. I want someone in this flat soon after that lamp is lit, regardless of the traditional meeting time."

"I'll have the place surrounded before you return, Holmes."

I happen to have a similar build to Owen's, so just in case Meyer was watching, Holmes thought it best that I go to the flat and give the signal and then meet Holmes and Lestrade back at Owen's apartment. In the meantime, Holmes walked to a nearby post office to send a telegram to Mycroft. By three o'clock, Holmes, Lestrade, and I were together again in Owen's flat, and Lestrade's men were covering the exits of the building and occupying other floors. Even Mycroft Holmes, in an almost unthinkable deviation from his routine, joined us in our vigil. We sat for hours in the little room, Lestrade and Holmes standing on either side of the door, and Mycroft and I sitting along the wall behind the bed, listening carefully to the other tenants going about their business.

Finally, at a little after nine, we heard footsteps slowly ascend the stairs and begin walking along the hallway toward the apartment. Lestrade and I drew our guns while Holmes brandished the loaded riding crop that was his weapon of choice. The footsteps halted at our door and before our quarry was able to knock a second time, Lestrade had pulled the door open. Meyer, however, was already holding a revolver in his hand, and it was pointed squarely at my head as the door swung open. In an instant, the loaded butt of Holmes' crop descended on the villain's wrist with a sharp crack, no doubt fracturing it and releasing his grip upon the pistol. As Meyer howled in pain and frustrated rage, Lestrade pressed the barrel of his gun to the spy's temple.

"Don't move, Meyer, as neither of my friends will hesitate to fire! Lestrade, is he alone?"

"Yes, Holmes. Come along, lads, and help me get this blackguard downstairs!" yelled Lestrade as several detectives descended the stairs to Owen's flat.

As we followed Lestrade and his captive out of the building, Mycroft ruminated, "Excellent work, Sherlock. Even if we have only prevented him from transmitting his most recently obtained information, he will make an excellent trade for any of our operatives that may have been captured as a result of this scheme."

"But what about his mysterious accomplice?" I wondered aloud.

"Yes, she may already be back on the continent," replied Holmes, "but if she isn't, we at least know what she looks like. And you have to admit, we did not do badly for three days' work. Now, I propose we make our way over to Nicholson's for a toast and a bite to eat, while Mycroft decides what we should tell Mr Pierpont."

The Adventure of the Missing Adam Tiler

I recall my friend Mr Sherlock Holmes once remarking upon the extraordinary occurrences that sometimes befall "when you have four million human beings all jostling each other within the space of a few square miles." In that case, it was after Commissionaire Peterson had introduced him to the first link in a chain of unusual events involving the theft of the Countess of Morcar's blue carbuncle, but time and again, we have witnessed what would seem the wildest of coincidences come together to form, with the aid of Holmes' uncanny insight and imagination, a picture as clear and coherent as crystal. Another such adventure began with a visit from one of the unlikeliest clients to have ever been received at 221B Baker Street. It was a Friday evening, and since my wife Mary was going to be away for several days visiting a friend, I decided to call upon Holmes after completing my rounds. I was greeted at the door by a beaming Mrs. Hudson who was eager for news of my life, and I must admit, I enjoyed commiserating briefly with my former landlady over the undiminishing eccentricities of her most notorious tenant.

"Last week, a courier tried to deliver several pounds of cormorant guano to him! It was for one of those experiments of his. You'd hardly credit it. 'Not in the house!' I told him. You should see who's up there with him now. A wrong 'un if ever I saw and up to no good, Dr Watson."

"Well, then I had best be on hand just in case," I said as I eagerly turned and ascended the seventeen steps to the rooms I used to share with Holmes. As I was about to knock, I heard Holmes call out from within.

"Please come in, Watson, I have someone here I would like you to meet."

I entered to find the sitting room unchanged with both Holmes and a blazing fire there to welcome me. It was satisfying to see the Persian slipper containing Holmes' tobacco still hung from the mantel, and his correspondence was impaled upon it as always with a jack-knife. As I greeted Holmes and took off my coat, a short and roughly dressed man rose from the basket chair by the table. He had a long, hooked nose and broad, toothy grin. I took his proffered hand as Holmes declared, "This is Mr Vinto Jones. I'd watch his hands, Watson, for you are in the presence of possibly the most talented pickpocket in the entire city."

"Well, bless you for a gentleman, Mr Holmes, and a pleasure to meet you, Dr Watson. There are precious few outside the trade as can appreciate the craft of it as Mr Holmes here, and Any old China of his is a friend of mine."

"Please, both of you have a seat. I trust you do not mind if Dr Watson joins us, Mr Jones."

"Not at all Mr Holmes, I'd be honoured. And if he can help me track down my old Adam Tiler, then the more the merrier."

Homes and I took our accustomed places in the two easy chairs by the fire, and I pulled a small notebook and pencil from my coat pocket. "So this is about a missing person? This Mr Tyler?" I asked.

At this, they both started chuckling.

"Ah, bless my soul! But, of course, he wouldn't, would he, Mr Holmes?"

"No, my friend Watson is an honest man and, much to his credit, has almost certainly never heard of an 'Adam'. You see, Watson, 'Adam Tiler', with an 'i', is thieves' cant for a particular sort of henchman."

"He holds the bread, you see. The routine is that I secretly hand my pickings to the Adam, quick as you please, before returning to my business. That way, should anyone, especially the Old Bill, suspect and try to search me, there's nothing to be found."

"It is a very common arrangement that goes back long enough that it has given birth to its own slang. Why don't you tell the story again from the beginning, Mr Jones, so that Watson can also be put into the picture," said Holmes as he leaned back in his chair and closed his eyes.

"As you please, Mr Holmes. Last Wednesday, my mate and I were down in Ravey Street near Mark Square. It was a fine day, and business was brisk. Late in the afternoon, I made my last dive, handed the proceeds to Adam, and we went our separate ways to reconvene in an alley by the butcher's shop around the corner on Blackall Street. Other people tend to avoid the spot, since it pongs a bit on account of the shop's offal. That made it a convenient spot to split the loot and for the Adam to change his clothes. You see, he always played posh, to make himself look less suspicious. To be honest, I think it probably came honestly to him. Anyway, when I arrived at our meeting place, he was nowhere to be found. I waited around for an hour, but he never did turn up. I've asked around after him at all our usual haunts, but no one's seen hide nor hair of him. It's not so much the bread and honey, Mr Holmes, I can make that up in a day–it's just that I'm worried about the lad. He's the first apprentice I've ever had and all. I can pay if you're willing to help me find him."

Holmes opened his eyes and gazed at Jones over his tented fingertips.

"No offence, Mr Jones, but I am not sure I can readily accept payment from you given your line of work. But let us not get into that just now. What was your associate's name or alias, and how did you come to meet him?"

"He went by Vernon Jule, so you tell me. I have no idea what his real name is. He sort of saved my life. I was diving over in Liverpool St, and one of the marks noticed his wallet was missing. He started raising an unholy racket and then pointed me out. Without thinking twice, I turned to drop the dosh into the pocket of someone beside me, but as I was finishing, I looked up to see the lad staring right down at me. I was sure I was done for, but before I could turn away, he smiled at me and winked. Then, he wandered off, while I, with utmost indignation, turned out all of my pockets for the angry gentleman and a bobby whose undesirable attention he'd attracted. After I had satisfied their curiosity and expressed my dissatisfaction at such shoddy treatment at the hands of all involved, I made my way to the Fancy Griffin pub. To my surprise, the lad fell in beside me along the way, introduced himself, and joined me for a few pints. He wouldn't go into detail, but he said he had fallen out with his old man and done a runner with some of the family's finest. That was a little over a month ago, and we've worked together ever since."

"Do you know where Jule was living?" asked Holmes.

"I've no idea. We started off at midday every day by meeting at that alley. If he's anything like me, his digs aren't really appointed for company."

"What did he look like?

"He was tall, almost as tall as you, Mr Holmes. About twenty-five years old, clean-shaven, and ginger. That curly red mane would stand out no matter the titfer. He could be dressed as a thief or a gentleman and carry himself as such. That's what made him so indispensable."

"Did he have any enemies? Could anyone be after either of you? Did you see anything unusual?"

"Perish the thought, Mr Holmes. Like I said, he was new to all this. As you know, I'm not and am always careful about not working on anyone else's patch. As for the rest, I saw a few of the regulars, beggars and shopkeepers, but no one unusual."

"Is there anything else you can tell me that might help me to locate this mysterious young man?"

"I'm sorry, Mr Holmes. I know it's not much to go on. There is one thing, though," he said as he produced a silver locket and chain from his waistcoat pocket.

"This was lying in the back of the alley where we were to divvy up the haul. It may be meaningless, but I'm positive this wasn't something I lifted. I also think I see a bit of a resemblance to him here."

Holmes took the opened locket from him and said, "It's a photograph of a mother with a small child, Watson. Do you mind if I hang on to this, Jones? Very well, I shall try to find your Adam Tiler. If I can lay hands on the man despite having so little with which to begin, it would be a feather in my cap. Where can I reach you?"

"God bless you, Mr Holmes. I'm staying above the Gilded Shoe Tavern in Shoreditch. Any message you leave with the landlord will get to me." And with that, Vinto Jones donned his cap and bid us farewell.

After he had departed, I asked Homes, "This could be an ugly business. Should you even be assisting a pickpocket, Holmes?"

"Yes, A young man from a wealthy family who has fallen in with criminals is more than a little vulnerable. As for Jones' status, arresting common divers is the business of the police. You and I have more important matters to pursue."

"How on earth do you intend to find this young man? You do not even have a name with which to proceed."

"I must admit, I am used to having a mystery at one end of a case, but to have one at both ends does create a challenge. But even if I am not up to that challenge, I have been at his game long enough to know at least one person who may be able to assist me in the matter. Can your wife and practice spare you for a few days?"

"Yes, that is what I came here to tell you. She is away for a few days, and I have already arranged to take a few days' holiday."

"Excellent, then we shall begin tomorrow. Tonight, we shall see what Mrs Hudson has prepared for us."

I stayed in my old room upstairs at Baker Street that night after one of Mrs Hudson's wonderful roast beef dinners. After I had dressed and had breakfast, Holmes having opted for a less conventional repast of coffee and cigarettes, we set out into the chilly autumn morning. Holmes had adopted his usual reticence, and I knew better than to intrude upon him while he was concentrating on the case in hand. There was a crisp breeze indicating that, despite the colourful leaves on the trees that were visible from our hansom as it passed St James Park, an impatient winter was fast approaching. Soon we were deposited before a club on St James Street that I immediately recognized as belonging to the notorious Langdale Pike. This society gossip monger was a columnist for several of the garbage papers, and Holmes could always rely on him to navigate the swirls and eddies of scandal within London's social scene.

A porter in livery led us to an oak-panelled reading room scantily populated by older gentlemen reading newspapers in sumptuous leather wingback chairs, but it was not in these chairs Pike was to be found. The journalist was seated in one of the bow windows at the farthest end of the room languidly smoking a cigarette with a long holder, watching the people bustling about below, like a velvet-jacketed bird of prey. He turned to us drowsily as we approached and said, "Ah, Sherlock Holmes and Doctor Watson. It is good to see you both. Better still if you have a story for me."

"Hello, Pike. I am afraid that it is I who am in need of your services today, but if you can help me, rest assured I will repay the debt."

With this, Holmes fed Pike, eagerly playing with the ends of his elaborate moustache, many of the details Jones provided the night before.

"You know, Holmes, if I had a penny for every well-to-do young ne'er-do-well who has been turned out of his house by his father…"

"You would have?"

"Precisely two shillings and thruppence…if we count only this month, and it is still early days. In any case it *is* your lucky day. The red hair is a dead giveaway–you are looking for Gavin Brayslow, son and heir to Lord Simeon Brayslow. The lad has always been work-shy, and the pater turned him out last month. The mother died years ago, and Gavin is the epitome of an only child. Rumour has it the boy helped himself to some of the family's silver on his way out. You will find Lord Brayslow at his home in Camden. Do promise to let me know how it all turns out, Holmes?"

Holmes assured him he would return after he had found young Brayslow, and we took our leave.

"Well, things are a little more straightforward now that we at least have a name to go with our description."

"Indeed, Watson. Pike has once again proven his worth. Let's telegraph Lord Brayslow now to see if we can arrange an appointment for this afternoon."

After we had posted the missive and emerged from the post office, Holmes hailed another cab and asked to be taken to Mark Square.

"I doubt there is much to be learned there, especially after the passing of several days, but I feel it would be remiss of us not to look over Brayslow's last known whereabouts."

We alighted into a square that was no less busy for being relatively small. People in heavy coats milled about, their frozen breath hanging in the hair as they spoke. The traffic thinned out somewhat as we turned onto Ravey Street and then Blackall Street. There we found several small establishments lining the sidewalks, including, in addition to the butcher's shop by the alley, a tea room, cigar shop, and several clothiers, all of which were quite busy. In front of the cigar shop, a stout man with a flat cap and wooden leg was selling the Morning Post. Holmes approached him and purchased one.

"By any chance, were you here last Wednesday evening."

"Yes, sir. I'm here every day, rain or shine," he said smiling.

"I am looking for someone," said Holmes as he fished a guinea from his coat and handed it to the man. "A young man, about my height with red hair."

"You've got to be joking. Look at all these people here. Sorry, but even if he had a paper off me, I wouldn't remember him."

Holmes nodded, and we strolled over to a blind beggar huddled on the ground beside his hat.

"Holmes, what could he possibly tell you?"

"Oh, Watson, you would be surprised," he said as he dropped another guinea into the hat.

"Were you here last Wednesday?" he asked the beggar.

"Aye, I'm here every day."

"I am looking for a young man who may have been here last Wednesday," he said as he nodded to me. I dropped a few more shillings into the hat, and he resumed, "About my height with curly red hair."

"Sorry, I don't recall anyone by that description. Perhaps, if he had been more generous, I might have noticed him."

"Well, this has been about as productive as I had anticipated. It looks like there is only one more possible regular to ask. I have saved the best for last," said Holmes as he looked toward a millenarian preacher, shouting fire, brimstone, and the end times from the opposite corner. My heart sank as I reconciled myself to approaching this lunatic with his bulging eyes and spittle flying from his lips as he ranted. His clothes were nice enough but ill-fitting, possibly donated. An opera hat that was slightly too small was pulled tightly down over his long white hair. He noticed our approach and focused his wild black eyes upon us.

"You, sirs. Would you hear the word of the Lord and learn about The Following? For the end is upon us, and there is little time in which to save your souls from everlasting damnation and the torments of Hell!"

"Actually, reverend, I am engaged in trying to save the soul of another. A young man of about my height with red hair. He may have been here last Wednesday."

"Only The Following can show you all the true way! I saw no such man last Wednesday, but when you find him, get you all to our church and learn the Truth. Here, take a pamphlet, and God willing, I will see you both at our new church tomorrow."

Holmes left it to me to take the pamphlet and extricate us from the man. Then, we made our way to the small alley by the butcher's shop that Jones had said was their rendezvous point. Despite Jones being quite accurate about the smell, Holmes dropped to the ground and began a minute investigation, but I could tell by his lack of zeal that he held out little hope. After twenty minutes, he sprang back to his feet, dusted off his knees and announced, "At least we can say we have done our due diligence here. The good news is that there are no signs of violence or a struggle, but that is only because there are really no signs of anything that might interest us. I suggest we return to Baker Street for lunch and to see if we have had a reply from Lord Brayslow."

As we were finishing our sandwiches and coffee, a messenger arrived with a telegraph from the young man's father.

"If you must come then do so at 2:00 pm."

"I know it is an impersonal medium, Holmes, but I would have expected him to sound a little more concerned."

"Still, we have received less courteous responses to our inquiries. I think there is just time for another pipe and a quick check of the papers before we go."

The papers yielded nothing, and I could tell Holmes was becoming concerned about the dearth of clues as we made our way to Lord Brayslow's home in Camden. I confirmed this by attempting to sound out Holmes in the cab.

"A name, a description, and a locket. Eh, Holmes?"

"Indeed, Watson. It is a meagre foundation upon which to build, is it not?"

"And the locket might not even be his."

"It may very well not. With some luck, maybe Lord Brayslow will shed a little light on the proceedings."

But Lord Brayslow was clearly not interested in discussing the business at all. At the neat, white stucco house, we were led to the library by a kindly and somewhat apologetic butler who insisted under his breath that the Lord really was concerned about his son. Lord Brayslow's behaviour, however, seemed to contradict this sentiment. A squinting, clean-shaven, old man, he did not rise from his desk upon our entrance and seemed to be more interested in the papers on it from which he barely glanced up. As we approached, I caught Holmes nod toward a framed picture on a shelf behind the desk. It was, without a doubt, the woman from the locket. Introductions were short and we were not invited to sit down.

"So what manner of trouble has the juvenile delinquent got himself into now? And do not think for a moment that I am going to spend a single farthing to rescue him. I gave him opportunities enough."

"As of yet, Lord Brayslow, we are uncertain as to your son's whereabouts. A concerned friend of his consulted me yesterday and says he has not seen him since Wednesday. I was hoping you might have some idea as to where he might be."

"I have not seen him in over a month, not since he made off with half the silver, the little toe rag. Must take after my wife's felonious brother. He was smart enough not to leave a forwarding address, though. If you do find him, please do tell him to remain out of touch. Good day."

"Thank you, Lord Brayslow, but there is just one more thing," said Holmes as he fished the locket from his waistcoat. "Do you recognize this?"

"What do you have there?" he said with a wince. "That is an old photograph of my wife and the boy."

"His acquaintance found it after your son had presumably left it behind. It *does* belong to your son?"

"It could, but I have to admit that I have not seen it before," he said as he returned it to Holmes having visibly softened. "Look...Mr Holmes. If you do manage to find the boy, please let me know."

With that, we took our leave.

"Where to now, Holmes?"

"Any suggestions would be welcome, Watson. There is simply no data."

And with that, Holmes sunk into one of his moods, and I could get nothing further out of him. He spent the remainder of the day sitting cross-legged and immobile in his easy chair by the fire, smoking plug after plug of noxious tobacco in his greasy clay pipe. When I awakened in my room and rolled over in the small hours, I could still hear the mournful sound of his violin from below. In the morning, I breakfasted as he, again, drank coffee and smoked a succession of cigarettes. It was as I was reading one the papers he had cast aside in frustration, that I was finally able to intrude upon his thoughts.

"Is it not always the way of things? You remember Filcote Hardiman, of course?"

"The notorious gang leader and extortionist. He is serving his sentence at Dartmoor," he brusquely replied.

"Yes, and there has emerged a movement, led by the prison chapelin, to free him early. Apparently, he has become quite religious and has even been ministering to the other prisoners. It is funny how so many only turn to religion after they have landed in the nick."

As I finished speaking, I raised my eyes from the paper and saw Holmes regarding me with a disturbing intensity.

"Watson, you may have just supplied the clue we need to find the missing young Brayslow."

"But Holmes, I fail to see how Filcote Hardiman can have anything to do with it."

"Not Hardiman, Watson. Hardiman's *behaviour*. As you said, it is a pattern we see time and again."

"But what does that have to do with our young man's disappearance."

"The locket, Watson. What if it does not belong to young Brayslow?"

"But it contains a picture of him and was found at his last known whereabouts. I fail to understand this train of thought."

"And yet I can imagine it all quite vividly," he muttered as he lunged from his chair and threw on his hat and coat.

"Do you still have the pamphlet the old man gave you yesterday?"

"Yes, Holmes," I said as I got up to retrieve it from my coat and hand it to Holmes who had already begun putting on his bowler hat and overcoat.

"I need to go out, Watson. Please wait here in case anything turns up."

Disappointed, I sank back into my chair and tried to resume reading the papers. On the other hand, it was nice to be once again ensconced in Baker Street, enjoying the nostalgia of the surroundings and Mrs Hudson's cooking while waiting on news from Holmes. Nothing did, in fact, turn up, though, and I retired for the evening with still no word from my friend. It would be late afternoon the following day before he finally put in an appearance, strolling into the flat and hanging up his hat and coat as nonchalantly as if he had only gone out for a walk around the block.

"Holmes, where have you been all this time?"

"I am sorry, Watson. I would have taken you with me but, as I was at that point only operating on a conjecture, was unsure as to whether I would need you to be on hand here in Baker Street."

"You need not worry on that score."

"Ah, well, if it is any consolation, I have located young Brayslow," he announced as he turned from warming his hands by the fireplace and leaned against the mantel.

"But how? Before you left, you were uttering some gibberish about Filcote Hardiman finding God and whether or not Brayslow was the owner of a locket that contained a picture of himself and his mother."

"Yes, Watson, but it was far from gibberish, for once again, you have proven yourself a great conductor of light. It was when you began trying to draw me into conversation with your account and observations on Hardiman that I caught the merest glimpse of a possibility. You will recall that, while we were questioning Lord Brayslow, he mentioned his son being like his 'wife's felonious brother'. It was when you mentioned the tendency of criminals to strongly embrace religion that I saw a thread on which to pull. I needed to begin gathering more data. My first stop was the church of The Following. I got the address from your pamphlet. I was in time for the second service, and what a production it was. The acoustics suited our reverend acquaintance from Blackall Street, and I could almost smell the brimstone in the air. I was seated behind one of the six attendees whom I gathered were also members of the cult, and at the end of the sermon, praised his performance to her and asked the reverend's name. It was Sidney Horrocks.

"I managed to slip out before Horrocks emerged to speak with his congregation and headed back to Lord Brayslow who confirmed that our reverend is indeed his wife's brother and had, in fact, discovered religion while still in prison for embezzling from the law firm at which he had worked. Watson, your flash of brilliance identified our man."

"So the locket belonged to the uncle, who was the lunatic preaching in the street? Incredible."

"There were other indicators. For instance, you will remember Vinto Jones stating that he saw 'no one unusual' in the square and 'a few of the regulars'. Surely, he would have recognized Horrocks as a regular and described him as something other than 'usual'. His being absent last Wednesday was irregular.

"My next errand was to make some arrangements with Vinto Jones. I headed to the Gilded Shoe and, upon his return, arranged to meet him in Blackall Street this afternoon. During the evening, I staked out the church of The Following in Hampstead. In addition to the church itself, an old gray stone structure dating back to the last century, there was a large residence that houses Horrocks and his fellow cult members and a few small outbuildings. Last night, after dark, Horrocks emerged from the house with a tray of food and a carafe, and entered one of these. It, too, was made of stone, windowless, and looked like a small shed. He left an hour later alone with the empty tray. Neither he nor anyone else visited the shed that night, but he did repeat the ritual this morning.

"This afternoon, I returned to Blackall Street or, rather, an alley around the corner from it. At the appointed time, Vinto Jones came to meet me with the good reverend's keys which he had lately borrowed while the man was terrifying passersby with great gusto just as we witnessed the other day. I made some quick wax impressions, and gave the keys back to Jones to, hopefully, return to Horrocks before he was the wiser. He is going to meet us here in a few hours to assist us with liberating young Brayslow."

"This is all utterly remarkable. But why has Horrocks abducted his nephew?"

"That we shall have to discover this evening. Now, I believe that is Mrs Hudson coming up the stairs, and unless I am mistaken, I can smell curry. I recommend supper and a brief nap before Jones arrives. We are going to have a crowded evening."

At eleven o'clock, Jones arrived and the three of us hired a growler to take us to Hampstead. The closer we got to the church, the more the traffic of the city began to thin, and by the time we arrived at our destination, there were very few people about. After we alighted from the cab about a block away, we began to walk slowly toward the church which took up the entirety of the next block.

"If last night's routine holds, Horrocks and the other zealots should be tucked up in the house by now, but be on the lookout nonetheless."

It was very cold and quiet, and the full moon painted the scene with a dim glow. There was a low, stone wall bordering the churchyard, and we followed Holmes as he shimmied over it and silently made his way across the frosty ground through the old, stunted headstones. There were three small outbuildings behind the church and the house, and Holmes began making his way toward the nearest of them. When we reached the shed, Holmes motioned for us to stand behind him as he examined the door's lock and produced some keys from his coat. He selected what he thought was the appropriate one and took a step towards the door to unlock it. At that exact moment, however, the door's knob began to turn and the door swung outward. Instinctively, Jones hid behind it as it opened while Holmes and I braced for what was to come next. It was Horrocks who emerged, and before the old man could utter a sound, Holmes had manoeuvred behind him, covered his mouth with his hand, and tackled him to the ground with one of the man's arms pinned behind him. I quickly removed my scarf and gagged the cult leader while Holmes produced some handcuffs. The three of us then entered the shed with our captive, and after Holmes gave a last look outside to make sure no one had seen, he noiselessly closed the heavy door behind us.

The stone building was musty with age and had a damp dirt floor. Within, illuminated by a single lamp hanging from a beam beneath the roof, sitting on the edge of a cot in his shirt sleeves with a blanket thrown over him and a chain leading from his wrist to the wall, was a tall, thin young man with curly red hair.

"Jones! Am I glad to see you! I hope you are as good at picking locks as you are at picking pockets. This lunatic has had me locked up in here for days. Who is that with you?"

"Master Jule, or should I say Brayslow. If you aren't a sight for sore eyes. I was so worried about you I went and hired Sherlock Holmes and Doctor Watson to find you."

Holmes produced another key and released Brayslow from his bond.

"And a good thing he did, but in the future I would strongly suggest you be a bit more selective about the company you keep, young man."

"You do not intend to involve the police, do you Mr Holmes?"

"Please do not be apprehensive on that score, Brayslow. Dr Watson and I are concerned with more weighty matters than apprehending pickpockets. If I were to truly administer justice in this case, it would be this reprobate I would hand over to the police. Please check his gag again, Watson, since we are going to be here for a few more minutes," he said as he turned again to young Brayslow with another key from his pocket and freed him from his chain.

"With the help of Watson, I was able to discover that it was your uncle who had abducted you and where he was keeping you, but I would very much appreciate it if you could fill in the details for me."

"I confess, I had no idea who he was when I passed him on the way to the alley, but he certainly recognized me. He followed and cornered me in the alley while I was waiting for you, Jones. Crying out my name and yelling about what a horrible sinner I was. Then he showed me a picture of my mother and said that if I did not let him help me to redeem myself, he would call the police. That he had heard all about my gambling and carousing. I was afraid he would give our whole game away, Jones. I decided it would be better to humour him, at least until we got to the church, but as soon as we got there, he coshed me. The next thing I knew, I was lying here with him looming over me ranting about all sorts of angels and demons and the various circles of Hell. I kept telling him I had repented, but he wouldn't credit it. Told me, when I was ready to stay with The Following forever, then he would set me free. I've been here for days! And what's worse, Jones, he took our dosh."

"Yes, it was the locket that helped lead us to you. He must have dropped it there. Well, you are free now, and I must ask you...What do you intend to do now that you are free. I should point out that your father provided me with information that helped me to trace you and would like to know that you are safe. I cannot say for certain, but returning to him seems to be your best course. No offence meant, Jones"

"None taken, Mr Holmes. Though I would hate to lose touch, I think he has a point. The son of a Lord should have an easier time of it than a pickpocket," said Jones sheepishly.

"You may have no worries on that score, gentlemen. I think I have had more than enough of youthful adventures."

"Very good. Then it is time we took our leave. If I or the Brayslow family hears from you again, Sidney Horrocks, rest assured you will be the worse for it," said Holmes

"But what exactly are we going to do with him?"

"That is simple enough Watson," he said as he advanced toward the reverend and started patting his pockets. He pulled out a key exactly like the one he was going to use to open the door and then produced the key to the handcuffs from his coat. He then blew out the lamp, and I heard a tinkle of metal as he tossed both keys into the darkness. With that we filed out, and he locked the door behind us with the key he had made, leaving Horrocks behind to find his own way outside.

After we had returned to Baker Street, having dropped off young Brayslow in Camden and having seen Jones off to Shoreditch, Holmes and I poured ourselves some brandy and sat down by the fire.

"I must say, Holmes, this visit to Baker Street certainly did not disappoint."

"Yes, I always enjoy our time together. As I have said, I am lost without my Boswell."

"Well, Mary is not due to return for another few days. Perhaps you will be visited by another worthy client before I go. Do you think young Brayslow really intends to reform?"

"Who is to say, Watson. He had not gone terribly far down the path toward the dock, and after all, there are worse criminals to fall in with than Vinto Jones. Judging by what he told us:

"'Consideration like an angel came
"'And whipt th' offending Adam out of him.'"

Showing admirable restraint, Langdale Pike never did publish the story and contented himself with some of Holmes' latest sidelights on the affair of the politician, the lighthouse, and the trained cormorant that he had managed to gather despite Mrs Hudson's protestations over his recent unsavoury deliveries.

The Politician, the Lighthouse, and the Trained Cormorant

I take a good deal of pride in my discretion and the trust my friend, Sherlock Holmes, places in me as a chronicler of our various adventures together. Holmes always assured his clients of my trustworthiness, and I have never betrayed anyone who agonised over the reputation or honour of a family member or friend with my pen. Nevertheless, recent attempts to get at and destroy my records of our cases may force my hand, as I stated in my recent tale of the Abbas Parva tragedy and its aftermath. If you are reading this now, please know that I do not take this step lightly and have been all but compelled to expose Sir Clive Blackstead as the first-class villain he is. This formal account has only been prepared by me with Holmes' approval as a last resort to finally defend both him and myself against this unscrupulous bounder and the various blackguards with which he freely associates.

It was on a brisk autumn afternoon when I, after the cancellation of my only remaining appointment for the day, decided to make a trip to Baker Street and pay Sherlock Holmes a visit. I pitied the poor hansom driver as a cutting, blustery wind seemed to blow right through my overcoat and threatened my hat as I sheltered inside his swiftly rollicking cab. Upon reaching my destination, I was immediately warmed by Mrs. Hudson's reception as she greeted me at the door of 221B. After catching up for a few moments and relentingly agreeing with her that I *did* understand that "he just was not the same when we were not living under the same roof," I made my way up the seventeen steps to the old sitting room. As I approached the door, he yelled from within, "Ah, Watson! Please come right in and help yourself to whatever's on the table." I immediately entered upon a scene so familiar it was as though I had never left. Holmes was leaning on the mantel by a roaring fire, reading a telegram while unopened trays containing the lunch Mrs. Hudson had prepared for him lay neatly untouched upon the table. As I poured myself some much needed coffee and began assembling a sandwich, he walked across the room and joined me at the table.

"As ever, your timing is impeccable, Watson. Though I still find it hard to forgive you for deserting 221B for matrimonial bliss, I suppose I should at least take comfort in the fact that you still seem to be able to join me at the beginning of so many of these little puzzles. But I jest, my good fellow. Tell me, does this not seem promising?"

He handed me the telegraph he had been reading, which I then read aloud:

"I should like to come this afternoon to discuss with you an extraordinary thing I found in a fish my Cassandra disgorged. Please reply. Andreas Georgiopoulos"

I then read it again and shook my head, "How extraordinary."

"Isn't it just? What do you make of it?"

"I have to admit that I'm having a hard time thinking about anything other than a woman 'disgorging' a fish. A

49

woman, named Cassandra, apparently," I said as I began chuckling.

Holmes threw back his head and laughed, "It does conjure a definite image at first glance, does it not?" After we had settled down, he continued, "But what else? Surely you noticed the sender's name is a Greek one? Does that and the reference to the fish and its 'disgorgement' not suggest anything else to you?"

I have to admit I looked at him blankly and chuckled some more.

"Greek fishermen are known for sometimes enlisting birds, specifically cormorants, as assistants. A snare is tied around the trained bird's throat–that way it can still devour smaller fish, but not a larger catch. When it does land a big fish that it cannot swallow, it returns to the fisherman and '*disgorges*' it. There is not much to go on here, but I think we are much more likely to encounter a cormorant, named Cassandra, when we meet Mr. Georgiopolous, than a gluttonous spouse or daughter. We'll find out soon enough as he's due here in about five minutes."

Not wanting to take the bet, I finished my sandwich while Holmes discarded his mouse-coloured dressing gown for a frock coat. Within a few moments we were addressing one of the most astounding pairs of visitors to have knocked upon the sitting room door.

"Greetings, Mr Georgiopoulos," said Holmes. "I see you have brought Cassandra with you. I am Sherlock Holmes, and this is my friend and colleague, Dr Watson. Please take a seat.

"I see you, too, are an avid fisherman and a shipbuilder. In fact, you seem to have been involved in almost every aspect of the craft. Note the calluses from the caulking mallet upon his right hand, Watson, not to mention those on the fingers of the left created by sewing sheets of canvas. Yet there are also shiny marks upon the rather expensive wool coat sleeves that suggest long hours at an angled drafting table."

"And, of course, you noticed the state of my favourite hat, the band of which has been sorely taxed, having had one too many lures stuck into it. I am overwhelmed that you have taken in my entire career at just a glance, Mr Holmes, but there's no denying it. I've been in love with ships and fishing my entire life, from my childhood in Greece to my autumn years in London. You see, I married an Englishwoman and moved here when I was a young man. Cassandra is the latest addition to the family."

Cassandra gurgled but remained perched on his shoulder as he sat down in the basket chair near the fire. She was a truly magnificent creature with dark gray plumage interrupted by white patches upon her head and breast and a yellow band near her beak. She seemed perfectly comfortable in her new surroundings.

"It was Galanis, the tobacconist, who recommended you to me. He also suggested how I should phrase the telegram to get your attention."

"Ah, yes. I've spent many hours and a good deal of money in his excellent shop. But please, tell us your story," encouraged Holmes as he sat down in one of the easy chairs with his fingers steepled and eyelids beginning to droop.

"Certainly, Mr Holmes. There really isn't much to tell. Cassandra and I like to fish along the coast when we can get away for a few hours, and last Sunday, I was fishing off Canvey Island while she ranged further afield. In fact, later on, she was out of sight completely for quite some time before returning with a large catch lodged in her mouth. Between you and me, it's just as well she couldn't swallow it. It was a sea bass, and they go through her, as you English say, like…well, you know the expression. After we returned home, as I was cleaning it, I found these lodged in its mouth and throat."

He reached into his vest pocket and retrieved two small brilliantly glittering objects and handed them to Holmes who made a long arm for a looking glass.

He let out a low whistle. "Two cufflinks made of eighteen karat gold," he observed as he examined them. "The letters 'C' and 'B' entwined on one and filled with diamonds and sapphires of the very best quality. The other is a match with the letters 'A' and 'T'. These are worth a small fortune. You are a very honest man, Mr Georgiopoulos. I wonder if the owner will appreciate it," he said as he handed the cufflinks to me.

Indeed, they were bonny things that seemed to emit gleaming sparks of white, yellow, and blue. Cassandra turned her head to look at them and gurgled again.

"Cassandra would most certainly tell us more if only she could, but I am afraid that's all I know, Mr Holmes. I was on my way to place an ad in the papers about them when I stopped by Galanis' shop. He thought you might be interested. If you are, I can offer a small fee. Given the circumstances, I wouldn't want to pay too much."

"What sort of person would I be if I charged an honest man for such an unselfish deed? We shall look into this, Mr Georgiopoulos, and will hopefully soon be able to tell you the whole story. May I keep these until then? Excellent. I assure you that I'll return them to you if we cannot ascertain the owner. I shall also credit you with their discovery if it turns out a reward has been offered. Then we shall be in touch with you. Good day, sir."

After showing Mr Georgiopoulos out, I tried to get Holmes to divulge his next steps, but all he would say about the matter was that he needed to do a bit of fishing, too. When I left him, he was still staring at the cufflinks and thinking. The next week went by with no word from him, and over the weekend my curiosity got the better of me. I visited Baker Street late Sunday afternoon and, even though Holmes had not yet returned, waited for him in the sitting room. I was comfortable in the familiar old surroundings–the Persian slipper by the mantel filled with his noxious tobacco, the correspondence affixed to the same with a jack-knife, the gasogene which prepared many a brandy and soda for a sorely tried client, and the deal table with all his chemical apparatus. I had just begun to doze off over the afternoon paper when Holmes arrived.

"Ah, Watson, I'm glad you've come. I believe I've figured out who's been so careless with his cufflinks. Help yourself to one of those cigars," he said as he hung up his overcoat and hat. Warming himself by the fire, he resumed, "I've been secretly shadowing our Mr Georgiopoulos. No, not because I suspect him of anything. It's Cassandra I'm interested in, but they're a package deal. I wanted to see if the bird has any favourite fishing holes. Georgiopoulos clearly only works part-time now at the Samiday Brothers Shipyard, which leaves him free to fish in the afternoons. That one spot on the coast in particular that he mentioned is an obvious favourite, and Cassandra seems to favour it, as well. We travelled along the Thames Estuary to Canvey Island last Tuesday, Thursday, and today, and while Georgiopoulos was taking his place upon the shore, I lingered on a tall dune in the background with my best binoculars. Every single time, after about an hour, Cassandra made a beeline to what is obviously her favourite spot far off shore. That is because two out of those three times, there was a large sailboat anchored there, and the owner was always generous about sharing some of his catch with her. Last Tuesday, she alighted on the stern of the boat, the *Persephone*, and waited for the man fishing there to come over with a couple of fresh herring. Cassandra is apparently extremely bright and well-trained. Normally, cormorant fisherman keep hold of the leash they tie around the bird's neck, but Georgiopoulos evidently trusts her enough to let her roam freely most of the time. She tried the same gambit again on Thursday, but the boat wasn't there. Today, she struck gold once more. I wonder if there isn't a more direct route for determining a bird's wanderings?

"What is even more interesting is the name of the *Persephone*'s owner: Sir Clive Backstead, MP for Wormesly Central, who is almost certainly the owner of the cufflinks."

"But how would his cufflinks wind up inside a fish?"

"It is hard to imagine such a thing occurring by accident, is it not? I'm currently following six lines of inquiry to ascertain the identity of 'AT' but haven't had any luck as of yet."

"You could simply ask him when you return the jewellery to him."

"Yes, but having gone this far, I would like to be able to see the complete picture. As you implied, it is odd to find one's cufflinks in a fish."

"This coming from a man who keeps his tobacco in a slipper," I chided.

"What is this?" he asked as his gaze rested upon the front page of the paper I had been reading. "'Unmanned Lighthouse nearly Causes Ship To Crash upon Rocks near Southampton.'"

"Yes, I was just reading that. It's right up your alley," I said before reading aloud, "'The group of passengers had chartered the yacht, *SS Paradiso*, from Mssrs Eastham & Cheswick for a day at the casinos in Deauville and were returning to Southampton when they found themselves almost dashed upon the crags at Pike Rock. According to both passengers and crew, the Pike Rock Lighthouse was both dark and silent. Had the captain been less capable, the results could have been disastrous. Fortunately, Capt Feargal Smiley knew the waters well enough to sense their danger in time and divert the yacht before disaster struck. As it stands, the ship only sustained some light damage to her hull.

"'The real mystery is the absence of the lighthouse's crew. According to Trinity House, the three keepers that had been working there came into the offices on Saturday to complain about having been replaced by a new crew without warning. The Brethren at Trinity House knew nothing of the substitution, but the original crew produced official paperwork they had been given by their relief indicating that they were all being reassigned elsewhere. This would be highly irregular, since it is customary for only one keeper at a time to be relieved when such a situation is necessary. The whereabouts of the relief crew are still unknown and the Brethren at Trinity House have pledged to get to the bottom of this mystery.'

"What do you make of it, Holmes?" I asked when I saw the keen look on his face.

"Can your practice and Mrs Watson spare you for a day or two? It appears Providence has offered us another line of inquiry."

"Yes, I can contact Anstruther today to see if he can step in as a *locum*, but what could this possibly have to do with Sir Clive's cufflinks?"

"Probably nothing, but it is worth exploring. Sir Clive is one of the Elder Brethren of Trinity House."

I only dimly began to grasp the significance of that simple statement and, as is usual, could get nothing more from Holmes that afternoon. After agreeing to meet at Baker Street in the morning, we parted company with him heading out to run an errand and me to make my arrangements and excuses.

The continuing frosty weather confronted us again as we hailed a cab the following morning. As we made our way south and then east through the tangled crowd of pedestrians, carts, buses, and other cabs along the Strand to Tower Hill, Holmes mentioned that he had paid a visit to his brother, Mycroft, yesterday evening at the Diogenes Club in order to obtain an introduction to the Brethren. I have mentioned elsewhere that Mycroft ostensibly audited the books for several government departments, but in actuality, sometimes *was* the British government. His word would no doubt grant us an ingress denied to many. The Brethren, three hundred Younger and thirty-one Elders, preside over Trinity House. Most come from maritime backgrounds and provide nautical advice to the government and administer charitable funds for the benefit of retired seamen, in addition to managing all the lighthouses of England, Wales, the Channel Islands, and Gibraltar. Our hansom soon entered the iron gates and deposited us before the arched doorway of the stately stone building overlooking the Tower.

A doorman in uniform greeted us and led us across rich oriental rugs through the hall filled with paintings of famous sailors and glass cases containing exquisite wooden models of famous ships. After passing through an arched opening flanked by alcoves containing model lighthouses that were actually lit and shiny green marble pillars, we entered another smaller hall with a wide staircase that branched to both left and right from its first landing. Our guide directed us to the right, and upon reaching the next landing, down a long corridor with oak doorways and Romantic paintings of nautical scenes at regular intervals. At one of these, he stopped, opened the door, and motioned for us to enter. A fastidiously dressed man with wavy hair and a rakish moustache, rose from a large desk and approached us.

"Mr Sherlock Holmes and Dr Watson, welcome to Trinity House. My name is Abelard Fanthorpe, and I'm one of the Elder Brethren. Your brother and I both frequent the Diogenes, Mr Holmes. Please, have a seat."

We both sank into luxurious leather armchairs by large wooden globes, one terrestrial and one sidereal, on each side of Fanthorpe's desk. After lighting our cigarettes, Fanthorpe asked what he could do for us.

"I would very much like to see the mysterious paperwork that was given to the original crew of the Pike Rock Lighthouse when they were relieved."

"Certainly, I had it retrieved earlier. Here you are," he said as he opened a long drawer in the middle of the desk from which he retrieved a slim packet of documents."

"Do you yourself see anything suspicious about them?"

"No, Mr Holmes. Other than that we have no record of the three crewmen that arrived at the lighthouse that day. Everything else is in order and, I have to say, bureaucratically routine."

"And the official signatures appear genuine?"

"Yes, but neither of those men recall having ever signed them."

"And this stationary with the House's letterhead and watermark is available to all the Elder Brethren."

"Naturally, Mr Holmes."

"Is Sir Clive Backstead in today?"

"No, but why do you ask?" he said, raising an eyebrow. "He's not one of the signatories."

"Is there an office that he uses when he is here? May we see it?"

Fanthorpe was obviously confused but rallied quickly.

"Yes, it's just down the hall," he replied and proceeded to lead us back out into the corridor. As we walked back toward the stairs, he stopped by one of the doors and unlocked it with a key from his waistcoat. The empty office was small with two green curtained windows, two desks, a small bookshelf, and wooden filing cabinets. Upon one of the desks sat an LC Smith typewriter, which Holmes began to examine, plucking at the strikers with his fingers and running his fingers over the reversed letters. Pulling a piece of stationary from a pile, he fed it into the machine and began to type.

"Aha! Watson, do you recall my mentioning that monograph I've been meaning to write on typewriters?"

"Yes, you said once that the type from a typewriter is as unique as an individual's handwriting. I'm guessing that this is the machine that typed those documents."

"It is indeed. Note the blurry bowls in the lowercase 'e's and 'a's and those faint finials. There's no doubt it's the same.

"Mr Fanthorpe, I'm afraid I must impose upon you. I need to turn these documents over to my brother's office and insist that no one enter this room until he has said otherwise. I apologise for any awkwardness this may cause."

"Please don't mention it, Mr Holmes, but would you mind telling me what it all means? That the documents would've been typed here hardly seems significant, in fact, that's precisely what I would expect. Did Backstead do something...dubious?"

"They were typed in his office, and yet he was not one of the Elders who signed the documents. Is that customary?"

"Well, no, I would have expected Rogers' secretary to have typed them, but why is that important?"

"Are there a limited number of typewriters in the building?"

"No, most administrative offices are equipped with one, but I must ask again…"

"As of right now, I don't have enough data to draw conclusions, but if I can eventually shed any light on this mystery for you, Mr Fanthorpe, I assure you I will do so. Thank you for your invaluable help."

And with that, we took our leave of the bemused Mr Fanthorpe and returned to our cab. As he climbed in, Holmes shouted the address of the nearest telegraph office and struck the ceiling twice with his stick. As we drew up to the curb, it seemed he bounded out before we had even stopped moving. In a few minutes he emerged, flourishing a telegraph.

"'AT'!" he shouted to me, smiling and then showed the cab driver the telegram. As soon as we were on our way, he explained.

"Yesterday, I telegraphed the office of Eastham & Cheswick, the firm that owns the *Paradiso*, to ask them if there was a passenger in the manifest with the initials 'AT', and if there was, to send me the name and address. Knowing this telegraph station was nearest to Trinity House, I asked for the reply to be directed here and held for me. This is their timely reply. We're now on our way to the West End to meet Miss Andrea Thesselthwaite."

Our driver stopped before a neat red three-story row house on a fashionable street in Mayfair that sat back from the sidewalk behind a short brick wall with an iron gate. In answer to our knock, a butler opened the door for us and took our card.

"Please tell her we would like to talk to her about the *Paradiso*," said Holmes.

The man took Holmes' card, disappeared into the house, and soon reemerged to lead us into the drawing room, which was warm and cosy despite the gray weather outside. A fire burned in the grate and fresh flowers adorned the various tables and piano. Miss Thesselthwaite was wearing an enchanting teal silk tea gown. Putting her knitting aside and sitting up from her couch, she greeted us cordially enough, though her apprehension was clear.

"Please, Mr Holmes and Dr Watson, take a seat, though I'm not sure how I can possibly tell you anything more about the accident than the crew of the yacht."

Holmes sat down in a wingback chair directly facing the woman while I sat off to one side in an easy chair.

"It must've been quite terrifying," said Holmes.

"I really didn't know what was happening at the time. I was talking to my friend, Phyllis, on the deck when the ship made a sudden lurch that knocked both of us off our feet. Sailors who had started running across the deck helped us up before running off again. Then there was another lurch and a horrible sort of grinding noise. It was only at that moment that I realised something was truly wrong. But within a moment, the noise stopped and we were proceeding along just as before. I hardly had time to be afraid."

"You were very lucky," said Holmes as he leaned forward in his chair. "Then, again, I suppose, if you'd been truly lucky, the lighthouse would've sounded its horn and lit your way far from those rocks. It is that which concerns me. That and the identity of 'CB'."

She paled a little at this and only said, "I'm not sure what you mean."

"Those initials are on this cufflink. We discovered Sir Clive Backstead trying to get rid of it," said Holmes as he held up the jewellery. "Here is its mate–'AT'. 'Andrea Thesselthwaite?'"

The colour had now gone from her face completely, and she replied, "Yes, Mr Holmes, I am ashamed to say you are correct. I gave those cufflinks to Clive as gift"

"Watson, I think perhaps a little brandy? Please Miss Thesselthwaite, you can rely on our discretion completely. Nothing will come out that isn't absolutely necessary. I am very much afraid that your life is in danger and need for you to tell me the whole story."

Taking a couple of sips of the brandy I offered her, she composed herself enough to speak.

"When I met Clive at Phyllis's party, that's my friend, Phyllis Dredgerton, that I just mentioned, I thought he was the most charming and interesting man I had ever met. There seemed to be no end to his accomplishments, and over the next three weeks, I accompanied him to dinner, the theatre, the opera, and a variety of social gatherings. Finally, Phyllis's husband, James, thought it was necessary to put me fully in the picture. I had no idea he was married, Mr Holmes. He wore no ring. I'm embarrassed to say that, at this point, I was rather infatuated and reluctant to break things off. No real harm had been done. But it was also, at right about this time, that things began to change. I had seen how cruel he could be to his staff and how little he thought of other people. He became more and more controlling. Insisting I wear certain clothes, act a certain way around his friends, and always trying to coerce me into doing things I'd no desire to do. When I committed what he deemed an infraction, he would become quite vicious. There was nothing for it but to break it off. Still, that wasn't the end. He would show up unexpectedly and threaten me to keep quiet, always accusing me of gossiping behind his back. Then, last week, he didn't appear at all. It is a habit I hope he never breaks, and I now understand why his wife does not come down to London."

"Did the darkened and silent lighthouse suggest anything to you?" asked Holmes.

"Yes, Clive is connected to Trinity House."

"Holmes, are you saying this was an elaborate attempt to murder Miss Thesselthwaite?"

"Given that she knew of Sir Clive's influence over the lighthouses, his intention was probably only to threaten, but it could have conceivably ended with several deaths."

Miss Thesselthwaite shuddered and drank the rest of the brandy from her glass.

"A pretty byzantine scheme to cover up an affair, is it not?" I asked.

"For a career politician? No. This scheme was probably no more complicated than any other for Sir Clive. A typed form and some signatures set all the wheels of bureaucracy turning, and people's lives hang in the balance."

"It wasn't just to hush up our relationship, Mr Holmes. Sir Clive was often indiscreet, particularly when he was drinking. Please do not ask me to be any more specific. I should only say it involved government business."

"Please say no more and do not worry. Watson and I now have what we need to ensure that he never threatens you again. I'll come around again in a few days to confirm that Sir Clive has been taken care of. Thank you for talking to us."

The next day found me again in Baker Street, having imposed upon Anstruther yet again. Holmes was hoping Sir Clive's routine from last week would hold and that we might be able to confront him. He had received a letter from Mycroft the day before with what he said were a few guidelines. I had picked up a yellow backed novel at a newsstand that morning, and was still reading it by the fire while Holmes sat in his chair and engaged in some rather hectic and impatient violin playing. At about three o'clock in the afternoon, Mrs Hudson brought in a telegram for Holmes, and he had jumped from the chair and plucked it from her hand before she'd had a chance to say a word.

"It's from Georgiopoulos. I asked him to notify us and Mycroft, if he spotted Sir Clive's sailboat in its usual spot. We should head to the docks."

We reached the bustling marina within the hour and had another hour's wait before Sir Clive's boat hove into view. Fortunately, a warm front had blown in with a light rain the previous night, and the sun was shedding a welcome, though still somewhat anaemic, warmth upon the docks while Holmes had been scanning the waters with his binoculars. The boat soon docked, and while the crew went about securing the vessel, Sir Clive, dressed in a pea coat with gray flat cap and flannel trousers, began to gather his catch and other gear. Holmes and I walked along the dock until we were beside the stern of the vessel.

"Sir Clive Backstead, I am Sherlock Holmes, and I would like to have a word with you about the business at the Pike Rock Lighthouse."

Sir Clive started, then scowled.

"I've heard of you. The second son. Some sort of detective, right? Well, I recommend you have a sniff around Trinity House or let your brother look into it. I don't know anything about it aside from what was in the papers."

"Oh, but I *do* know something about it," said Holmes as he held up one of the bejewelled cufflinks in each hand, "and it would be in your best interests to discuss it."

Sir Clive's eyes widened briefly, but he quickly regained his composure. He then hastily descended from the boat to the dock and walked over to us.

"What do you have there, Holmes? They're very pretty, but I'm not sure why you're flashing them at me in such a dramatic fashion."

"It won't do, Sir Clive. I know they are yours, partly because they bear your initials, 'CS'. It was an eccentric way of disposing of the evidence of your affair, but you stuffed them into the mouth of a sea bass, which you then fed to a cormorant, from which I was able to recover them. I've also shown them to

Miss 'AT', Andrea Thesselthwaite, who confirmed that she gave them to you."

"B-b-but how? If it were a different time, you'd be accused of witchcraft. No one could've observed me that day, n-not even the crew," he sputtered.

"It is my business. I also examined these forged documents from Trinity House and found out they were typed on the typewriter in your office there. The police are still searching for the three fake keepers, which should make this chain of evidence so complete that even the most inept prosecutor could obtain a conviction."

Sir Clive was visibly shaking, and I half expected him to either start running or hurl himself at us.

"But we shall leave that for now. Please restrain yourself, sir. We're not here to clamp you in irons. I'll settle for your word that you'll never bother Miss Thesselthwaite again. Do I have it? Good. Though Trinity House won't have anything more to do with you, I know that several of our friends in Whitehall will soon be in touch. You may be able to evade what I'd consider justice this time, but you have earned the constant scrutiny of both myself and my brother."

We all followed Holmes' gaze as he looked over his shoulder at the hulking man regarding us from a park bench further down the dock.

"Were I a criminal, such as yourself, I would fear that much more than the police."

I followed Holmes as he turned his back on the MP and walked away.

"Come, Watson. There is a pub around the corner that does an excellent Tweed Kettle. We can celebrate the end of this case there."

"But Holmes, should we really have let him go like that?" I asked, trying to hide my disappointment.

"I don't like it either, but I'm afraid a higher authority has taken the matter out of our hands, my friend, and Scotland Yard's, too, no doubt. Evidently, an embattled Sir Clive would be a political liability, but a compromised Sir Clive is a potentially precious asset. Cheer up. I sincerely doubt Sir Clive will ever be a threat to anyone again."

"What about Mr Georgiopoulos?"

"I shall return the cufflinks to him and tell him that he's welcome to them. A bad end to a torrid affair. The owner wants nothing to do with them, *et cetera*. Perhaps if we're lucky, he'll reimburse us for our luncheon," he said with a sly smile.

The Adventure of the Silver Band

I feel I have been very fortunate to have had a chance to accompany my friend, Sherlock Holmes, on so many extraordinary adventures, some of which I have managed to chronicle in various periodicals. Though Holmes himself is often critical of my approach to these narratives, I feel that, at the very least, I have presented an accurate depiction of the abilities and methods of the world's first consulting detective that can be preserved for posterity if fate allows. Holmes himself has even referred to me, tongue planted firmly in cheek, as "his Boswell", and this, I feel, is really my role in our unusual partnership. Holmes, though, has been kind enough to embellish this by saying to me, "It may be that you are not yourself luminous, but you are a conductor of light. Some people without possessing genius have a remarkable power of stimulating it." It was, I am reasonably certain, a genuine attempt at a compliment and, in keeping with Holmes' nature, was inarguably accurate: a sounding board, my other role. There was an occasion, however, about fifteen years into our association, when I had the opportunity, albeit briefly, to turn the tables.

It was early in the summer, and the sun had finally set on a warm evening in Baker Street. A slightly balmy breeze still stirred the floral curtains of our sitting room and swirled the clouds of smoke from our pipes with its invisible tendrils. Holmes was just beginning to mention some of the peculiarities of the sagas of Orkney when the bell rang downstairs. There was a brief commotion and then the sound of feet upon the stairs. Holmes tilted his head and stood.

"Two men, and one is our friend Lestrade. Inspector Lestrade, do come in. No need to knock," exclaimed Holmes as he crossed the room and opened the door for our two visitors.

In the doorway stood the Scotland Yard detective, his face still somewhat sallow despite the summer sun and looking particularly keen and slightly mischievous as he removed his bowler hat. He was accompanied by a young, blond-haired man in a light brown suit and boater. An obviously recent, darkening bruise coloured his left cheek.

"Good evening, Mr Holmes and Dr Watson. This is Geoffrey Dulisle, a clerk at Dulisle's Fine Wines and Spirits in Waterloo. He has just experienced an unfortunate incident at work that the Yard wouldn't normally have much time for, but that I think you, with your interest in the bizarre and unconventional, may wish to hear about."

"You intrigue me, Lestrade. Come, have a seat, and tell me, Mr Dulisle, of this incident that has occurred at your family business with which you are bored and often resentful."

"That the shop is owned by my family is obvious from its name, but how in the world can you presume to know my attitude toward it, Mr Holmes?" asked Dulisle as he settled into the basket chair.

"There is a book by Robert Louis Stevenson in your coat pocket. Obviously, Lestrade would have conducted you here directly after you received your injury. That means you brought the book with you to work, and that suggests boredom. The forefinger and middle finger of your right hand are stained a dark orange from cigarettes, and yet your clothes bear hardly any odour from the tobacco. This suggests that you've been doing your smoking outside the shop instead of working, indicating detachment or resentment. Finally, what young man doesn't get bored with and resent having to work in the family business?"

At that, the young man smiled along with Holmes and chuckled.

"I'll admit, it's a fair cop, but I do enjoy it sometimes, as well."

"Please tell us more about your experience at the shop today and omit nothing," said Holmes as he sank into the easy chair, lit his oily clay pipe, and assumed the languid attitude he so often took on when listening to potential clients recite their narratives.

"It was rather slow tonight, and I was taking inventory while my father was working in the office behind the counter. A man walked in who seemed suspicious to me, because despite the warm night, he had a ragged scarf wrapped round the lower part of his face and a wide brimmed hat pulled down low over his head. He was also wearing gloves, but he removed these as he retrieved a large bottle of whisky from one of the shelves. As I watched him, he looked around to see if he was observed, but obviously didn't spot me. Slipping that bottle into a coat pocket, he grabbed one more, and I quickly ran around the shelves to meet him at the exit just as he reached it. I collided with him and grabbed both of his wrists while calling for my father. As I did so, the scarf slipped down, and I could plainly see the man's face," he said, trailing off for a moment.

"Did something strike you about the thief's appearance?" asked Holmes.

"Mr Holmes, the man's skin was completely blue. Face, ears, eyelids–all blue. I must have relaxed my grip in surprise, for he was able to free his right hand, which was empty, and strike me with the heel of it before I could restrain him again. With that, he was out the door like a shot, and I ran out behind him yelling for the police."

"And this is where I come in," interjected Lestrade. "I happened to be just around the corner at Johnson's newsstand– he's assisting me with nabbing some extortionists–when I heard the cry and ran over. A patrolman soon joined us, but the thief had already fled into the night."

"Is there anything else you can tell me about the man?" asked Holmes

"Nothing much as stands out. He was a little taller and heavier than me, with short dark-brown hair, moustache, and brown eyes. I reckon he was about forty-years-old. I did see his hand particularly clearly as he struck at me, and even that was blue. Not just the top, but the palm and skin beneath the nails. He was dressed in a ragged, brown tweed jacket and gray flannel trousers."

"And this blue colouring was uniform and not splotchy, like one might expect from makeup? Exactly what shade of blue?"

"Yes, it looked like it was his normal skin colouring and nothing rubbed off on me. It was a dark, silvery blue."

"This is most gratifying," whispered Holmes, and I cleared my throat.

"Did you see where the man was headed?"

"No, Mr Holmes. He ran straight across the street and into a crowd. I can't tell you in which direction he headed."

"Thank you, Mr Dulisle, and thank you, Lestrade, for introducing us to such an extraordinary character."

"So, you're interested?" asked Lestrade, raising an eyebrow.

"Oh, yes. I shall be in touch. Mr Dulisle, I hope to be able to tell you more about your attacker soon."

After our guests had taken their leave, Holmes immediately retrieved his commonplace book and began flipping through it at his desk after filling and relighting his pipe. I left him to it, knowing there was no real alternative, and pulled a few medical reference works from my shelf. I spent an unproductive hour or more sitting on the couch, trying to find some entry or article that could shed some light on that criminal's bizarre skin colour. My eyes finally glazed over, and I refilled my pipe while regarding Holmes, who had just emitted a frustrated sigh and stood to retrieve yet another volume from his shelves. There was something just out of reach, nagging at me from the back of my mind, some syndrome or side effect. Something seen briefly when I was a student.

It finally dawned on me. I picked the first reference book I had consulted back up from the floor and turned to the beginning. Relishing this chance to reverse our customary roles and be the one performing the dramatic revelation, I carried the book over to Holmes' desk, laid it open before him, and tapped the page with the relevant entry.

"Not just blue, Holmes. He specifically said 'a dark, *silvery* blue'. *Argentum*."

Holmes read the entry, "Argyria. A condition caused by excessive exposure to the element, silver, or chemical compounds thereof. The dominant symptom of argyria is a permanent transformation of the skin colour to a grayish or silvery blue. It occurs in people who ingest or inhale silver in large quantities. It can also be caused by the application of silver to the skin."

"And silver has been used, controversially, to treat a variety of infections, skin conditions, sinus problems, and stomach complaints," I added. "It's snake oil peddled by quacks, which means we may be able to trace the thief through his doctor."

"Watson, you have exceeded yourself," said Holmes in genuine admiration. "You can further amaze me by telling me you know of just such a quack operating nearby."

"I don't, but I know just whom to ask. There will almost certainly have been more than one victim. Tomorrow morning, I shall contact several of my colleagues and encourage them to make enquiries of their colleagues. Hopefully, someone will have seen a blue patient complaining about their prior physician."

"Then I shall leave the case in your hands, my friend."

And with that we each retired to our rooms for the evening. In the morning, I telegraphed several physicians whom I knew well before heading to my practice. When I returned to 221B Baker Street, a small stack of telegraphs awaited me, which I immediately sat down to read. I was starting to despair when I finally found the answer we had been seeking. This time, I resumed my normal habit of reading aloud to Holmes who was anxiously smoking a cigarette at the table across from me.

"It's from Jackson, my occasional *locum*. 'Farmingdale, dermatologist, told story of blue victim of Dr Elias Chadbutter. Quack with fad for colloidal silver in East End.' It's a shame he doesn't have the address."

"Please do not worry on that score, Watson. I think I know just the man to tell us that and even more if this Chadbutter is in the habit of treating criminals. But it's early yet, and you're probably famished. Mrs Hudson should soon be up with our dinner."

The late setting sun found us in a hansom cab making its way along Commercial Road in the East End. After entering Limehouse, we soon found ourselves in a warren of dirty, narrow streets, and Holmes pounded the ceiling of the cab with his cane to stop the driver.

"It is better we go the rest of the way on foot. Did you remember to bring your revolver?" he asked, and I nodded my head before getting out. After Holmes had paid the driver, he began walking very deliberately, head down, glancing both left and right from under his bowler. There was very little illumination and a fog had blown in, but I could occasionally make out the shapes of some idlers, all apparently in various stages of intoxication.

"It is not a neighbourhood I would recommend visiting alone, Watson, even in daylight, carrying a firearm. Though *some* authors have made much of the Chinese and opium dens in Limehouse, being so near the docks, it is truly an international zone of iniquity. Note the absence of older women, children, or even vendors."

"Actually, Holmes, I did just see a woman back there…Oh."

Not only would I have been concerned about the denizens of this underworld if Holmes had not been by my side but I am fairly certain I would never be able to navigate my way out of it. We had made so many turnings, I had lost track of our direction, and no stars looked down upon the silent menace of this vile neighbourhood. This silence was finally broken by the slamming of a door as a man fell howling to the pavement, both hands thrown up over a face streaming with blood.

"We have reached our destination. Welcome to The Parson's Regret," he announced as we approached the double doors that had just slammed shut in the corner entrance.

"I'd keep your hand on your gun," he said, pulling the right door open and passing through it into the dark, smokey pub. Joyless music tinkled from an out of tune piano as a young woman swayed over it, eyes half shut, striking dully at the keys. The rest of the haggard clientele occupied some of the small tables scattered about and a few of the barstools. I followed Holmes over to one of the menacing private booths on the left, trying to reassure myself that what I smelled was only the filthy taps. As I did, I could have sworn a small man in a dirty pea coat and flat cap made eye contact with Holmes, but it was just for an instant. A large sweaty man with prodigious sideburns and a filthy apron soon appeared to take our order of ale. I followed Holmes' lead and we drank in silence after the bartender returned. We had another round in front of us before the little man I had observed earlier quickly swung himself into the booth beside me.

"Good evening, Mr Holmes. Mind if I join you?" he whispered in a way that we could clearly hear, but I realised would have been inaudible to anyone else.

"You're just the man I've come to see. Dr Watson, this is Leggett. He knows things other people don't and is sometimes willing to put me in the picture, as well."

"That's right, Mr Holmes. Just as long as it don't involve nothing that will end up in court. It would be all my life's worth if any of these fine gentlemen thought I was some kind of nark of the police. You'll be happy to hear my rates have remained fixed. Well, bless you for a gentleman," he said, deftly pocketing the coins Holmes slid to him across the table.

"I'm looking to enlist the services of a medical man, a Dr Elias Chadbutter. What do you know of him and where might I find him?"

"He's a bit of a kook, Mr Holmes, a long-haired charlatan who's been taking too much of his own medicine, if you know what I mean. But he knows how to cut out a bullet, and he knows how to keep schtum. Lives above his practice in the middle of Portsmouth Lane."

"Excellent, thank you. Please, help yourself to this round of drinks. Watson and I haven't touched them. Now, quickly and discreetly, Watson. Good evening to you, Leggett." he said, as we slipped out of the booth and back into the night.

"An interesting character is Leggett. He was facing a considerable term in prison for robbery when I caught the actual guilty party. He has been a reliable source of information ever since."

"It's a pity he can't find a nicer local." I said as I put my hand back into my coat pocket.

Soon we emerged from that dank maze into a different kind of squalor. We threaded our way through various pedestrians who were on a broader spectrum of class and sobriety, and though it was getting late, the streets still rang with sounds of cabs and carts. From Limehouse, we soon made our way to Commercial Road, and a few more turns brought us to Chadbutter's practice on Portsmouth Lane. It was a forlorn and begrimed two-story rowhouse, huddling between a somewhat fragrant butcher's shop and a particularly depressing pawn shop, featuring such choice items as a cracked wooden leg and various unmatched shoes in its front window.

"It's a shame we didn't arrive sooner. We could've gone for a shop," quipped Holmes as we approached the dark house.

"If we return for the leg, perhaps they'll throw in a shoe for free," I replied.

Holmes rapped on the door of the practice, but there was no sound from within. After a few more knocks, he gently turned the knob, and the unlocked door swung open. We quickly entered and shut it behind us. The only illumination was from the gas lamp outside filtered through the grimy front window and its disintegrating chintz curtains. Holmes called the doctor's name a couple of times, but the house was almost unnaturally still. Holmes and I entered the narrow hall, and he stopped to light an oil lamp on a small table along the wall. When he lifted it a shape became visible on the floor several feet in front of us.

It was a thin man with long, stringy hair and glasses, who was quite dead. The ligature marks around his neck were visible even from a distance in the poor lighting, and a large pool of blood had collected around his head. I kneeled down to get a better look, and Holmes went around the other side into the large room, which was Chadbutter's examination room.

"He's been garrotted," I announced. "The murderer used so much force that he cut into the neck and severed the jugular vein."

Holmes turned up the gas in the practice room and then dropped down on all fours to examine the floor. He placed his hands just above the surface as if he was creating a frame with his fingers.

"We're lucky Chadbutter didn't employ a char. There's just enough dust on this floor. There were four of them, lined up here and shifting. They were turning as Chadbutter backed towards the door. Watson, please hold still."

He made a short leap to the left of the body behind me and retrieved the lamp.

"And he was backed into the arms of his killer. I'm sorry, but we passed a bobby a couple of blocks back. Could I please impose upon you to fetch him?"

I soon found the policeman, and upon hearing what we had found, he blew his whistle for assistance. By the time we had returned to the house, he had been joined by two of his comrades. I took the liberty of asking one of them to summon Inspector Lestrade from the Yard if possible. Holmes was waiting in the hallway to show them the body and keep them from disrupting the scene. He then disappeared further into the house, turning on the gaslights as he went from room to room.

After about an hour and a few minutes after Holmes had rejoined us, Lestrade arrived. We greeted each other warmly despite the grim circumstances. Holmes then brought him up to speed on the case and began to lead him and me back into the hall.

"He lived in the rooms at the top of that staircase on the right, but his practice is just back here. Watch your step. As you can see, Watson's deduction was absolutely correct. Here's a salve of colloidal silver. There's a whole case of the stuff. Regrettably, there's little else to go on."

"We'll make a detective of you yet, Dr Watson," joked Lestrade. "As for your friend, though…"

We exited the examination room and entered Chadbutter's office which was next door to it.

"His appointment book is on his desk. There's nothing in it to suggest he anticipated being visited by a party of assassins today. There are certainly no notes about patients suddenly having turned blue on him. The other rooms were equally disappointing."

"Did you discover *anything* else during your search, Holmes," asked Lestrade. "If not, my men and I will make a proper one."

"Just more evidence of the visit of the five men, their heights, weights, style of boots. I've written it down for you here. It's certainly not enough to track them down, but I do have a plan. If you don't mind giving us a lift back to Baker Street when you're finished with your own search, I'll go over it with you and Watson so that you can give me your opinions."

Despite his boasting, Lestrade was equally unlucky, and after posting one of the bobbies at the door of the house and giving instructions to the others, he ushered Holmes and me into a Scotland Yard growler. Along the way Holmes outlined his plan to advertise in several newspapers my "new miracle cure for all afflictions of complexion, including but not limited to extreme discolorations". This remedy of mine was certainly news to me, but I assured Holmes I could come up with some sort of convincing placebo. Then we would wait at my practice to see if any of the crooks would take the bait. It seemed sound enough, but I was a bit concerned that my published accounts might give away the game.

"I think it's a chance we'll have to take. It's far more likely that they'll ask about where you're located and how long you've been there. I don't want to risk losing that authenticity on the off chance that they're dedicated readers of popular periodicals. If this doesn't quickly bear fruit, I have two other approaches we can take."

"It's an unorthodox approach, Holmes," Lestrade chimed in. "But your unusual methods do sometimes prove fruitful in odd cases, like this. I'm willing to give it a go."

Two days later, an unusual man entered my consulting room. His clothes were dishevelled and downright dirty. A slouch hat covered most of the upper part of his face, and a tattered scarf concealed the rest.

"Sorry to trouble you without having made an appointment first, Doctor, but I saw your advertisement in the

Daily Telegraph about your cure for ones suffering from skin troubles."

"Oh, I'm so glad the word is getting out. I take it you suffer from some problem with your complexion?"

He closed the door behind him, and removed his hat and scarf.

"See for yourself."

He stood before me like something out of an Edward Lear poem, the skin on his head completely blue. Like Dulisle described, it was as if he had been born that way. I asked him to disrobe and observed that the effect was uniform. His entire body was a silvery blue, and his hygiene quite deplorable. There were signs of a recent staphylococcus infection in addition to his bizarre hue. After he had gotten dressed again, I directed him to take a seat in the easy chair beside my desk.

"How did this happen, Mr...?"

"Smith, John Smith. I've suffered some recent misfortunes and, as you've probably guessed by the state of me, have had to resort to sleeping rough on most nights. The infection you noticed set in, and made me so miserable I had to see a medico. I found a man in the East End who prescribed a salve. He said it was some sort of mixture of silver and honey. The infection got better, but now I look like a circus freak. Some of my mates who've been dossing in the same place suffered similar."

I thought I would gently try to pry some more information from the man.

"Where are you and your friends staying that is so filthy and couldn't you find better?"

"I'd rather not say, sir. A few of us have had to break the law on occasion–just to survive, sir, just to survive, I swear. I promised them I wouldn't nark. Surely, you can understand?"

"Indeed. And the doctor you saw?"

"Some foreign chap off Commercial Road. Disappeared like a thief in the night."

"I see. Well, I do think my new treatment will help. Excuse me, while I retrieve the pills for you."

"But, Doctor, what about my four mates? I don't suppose you could provide me with enough medicine for all of us."

"Normally, I would want to examine all of you first, but obviously you're all going to need to be cured as soon as possible if you're to improve your prospects. It would also be edifying to see five successes from my new treatment. I'll be right back with enough for you all," I said as casually as possible and left the consulting room. I walked up the hall to my small study and went inside. Holmes was standing behind the door. I retrieved the pill bottles from the desk drawer and nodded silently to him.

I returned to the consulting room to find Mr "Smith" still sitting by my desk. He eagerly took the bottles of sugar pills from me and listened carefully to my instructions for taking the placebo. I have to admit that, for just a moment, I almost felt sorry for this pathetic creature but then remembered Chadbutter lying there on the floor. He took his leave, promising to return to show me the results. When I heard the outer door shut, I returned to my study. As planned, Holmes had already departed, hopefully on the trail of the blue man.

That evening, I returned to Baker Street and was soon joined there by Lestrade. We had just partaken of one of Mrs Hudson's excellent roasts and were drinking coffee when Holmes finally arrived.

"Your patient went well out of his way to visit you, Watson," said Holmes as he took a seat and poured some coffee. After lighting his oily clay pipe, he continued, "I think this new career avenue you're pursuing will prove quite fruitful."

"At least those sugar pills won't cause anyone to dramatically change colour," I replied.

"Where did the man lead you, Holmes?" asked Lestrade impatiently.

"The whole way back to Limehouse. More specifically, to an abandoned sawmill near Limehouse Pier. Like his colleague at Dulisle's, he did a little light pilfering on the way back, but that's probably immaterial in light of the murder charge and the rest."

"The rest?" asked Lestrade.

"Yes, after I found his hideout, I waited for it to get darker, so I could get a look at his confederates. The building is a ruin, so finding a spot from which to observe the gang from outside was a simple matter. I crept up to a sizable hole in one of the clapboard walls and was able to see them all quite clearly as they sat around a fire. Do you remember the botched robbery of the South Central Savings Bank, Lestrade?"

"Yes, that's a hard one to forget. The Arbegast Gang wasn't it? They'd no sooner asked everyone to put up their hands when a trio of stevedores tackled four of them, and the alarm sounded. They shot and killed one of the labourers and promptly fled in a panic without getting a single dime. The guard identified the gang's leader when his mask was yanked off in the scrum. Is that whom we're dealing with? We've been on the lookout for them for the past few weeks."

"None other. If their skin had broken out into pink and purple polka dots, I would've recognized them. Still, that silvery blue skin is a shocking sight. I would say it has ruined their bank robbing career if their sheer incompetence had not already accomplished that," he said, chuckling. "But I can see you're impatient, Lestrade. We can depart as soon as I have finished my pipe. They were passing around a large bottle of gin when I left, so they should be easy pickings for you and your men.

"Watson, I've already got my revolver in my coat. You would be wise to bring yours, as well."

Four of Lestrade's men had been sitting in a growler outside 221B, and Holmes, Lestrade, and I piled into another after Holmes had given the driver the location of our destination. Once more, we found ourselves racing through the darkened city headed east. Driving a few blocks past our destination, our carriages stopped in the shadowy Limehouse Causeway, and the seven of us disembarked, quietly navigating our way through the grimy streets by the light of anaemic gas lamps down to the docks. At the end of a row of warehouses stood a large two storey wooden structure in an advanced state of dilapidation. The middle of each of its two gables sagged, and its smokestack had crumbled to the ground. Even at our distance, gaping holes in the clapboard walls were visible.

When we got within fifty yards of this building, Holmes drew his revolver from his coat pocket and said, "Wait for me while I check to see if the coast is clear. I'll wave if it is."

For several tense minutes, we watched Holmes walk silent and cat-like up to those crumbling clapboard walls of the mill. No light from inside was visible to us, and apart from the lapping of the Thames, the only sounds we heard were the occasional scurry of a rat or shout of a distant reveller. Holmes' silhouette was just visible in the light of the waning moon as it reached the wall facing us. As he waved, we drew our guns and descended on the mill as quietly as we could. Holmes moved a little further along the wall and motioned for us to follow him around the corner of the building. When we reached him, we could see that he had found a hole large enough for each of us to pass through if we stooped. He entered first and waited while we followed him one-by-one, guns drawn. What had not been removed from the vast interior, hung broken, rotted, or rusted from the cobwebbed walls and ceilings. In the middle of the dirt floor were five men in filthy bedrolls lying around a dying barrel fire. We instinctively began surrounding the band of men, and once we were in position we began walking slowly toward them. We had gotten within fifteen feet of the sleepers when one stirred and then bolted upright, thrusting his hand into his trouser pocket. Lestrade cried out.

"Inspector Lestrade of Scotland Yard! Get your hands in the air! You're surrounded!"

The man who first spotted us froze, hand still in his pocket. Three others started and quickly shot upright with their hands above their groggy heads. The last one rolled over brandishing a revolver. Lestrade fired once, and the man's head snapped back as if kicked. He would not rise again on his own. The man with his hand in his pocket, mouth hanging open, slowly removed and raised it. Getting over their initial shock at the gang's bizarre appearance, Lestrade's men produced their handcuffs and got to work.

"I'm arresting you for the attempted robbery of the South Central Savings bank and the murder of one of the men who attempted to stop you," crowed the short Inspector.

"And for the murder of Dr Chadbutter, Lestrade," interjected Holmes. "Note the boots and other details I mentioned the other evening. If you search these men now, I have no doubt you'll find a garotte on one of them."

At this point, the man who had visited my practice noticed me and said, "What are you doing here? You were in on this?"

"It is from Dr Watson's practice that I followed you back here," said Holmes.

"But I never saw anyone following me?"

"That is what you may expect to see when I follow you."

"Then the pills?" he asked dejectedly.

"Sugar pills. I'm afraid your condition is incurable," I said.

"But you won't have to suffer long. These are hanging jobs," crowed Lestrade.

And with that, the policemen cuffed the men and stood watch or searched, while Holmes, Lestrade, and I returned to retrieve the carriages.

"So you're sure that these men also did for Chadbutter?" asked Lestrade as we walked.

"They match my physical descriptions, and they certainly had a motive for revenge. The last thing an aspiring bunch of bank robbers wants is for everyone to recognize them instantly."

"Very good. If the garotte's in that mill, we'll find it. Once again, I owe you my thanks."

"Please, don't thank me, Lestrade. It was Watson who made the initial deduction that led us to Chadbutter, and he is also responsible for leading us to the gang's hideout."

"And thank you, Dr Watson," said Lestrade, shaking my hand.

"You're most welcome, Lestrade, and rest assured, my name need not appear in the matter," I replied, laughing before climbing into the carriage.

Sure enough, the garotte was discovered, and a second charge of murder was added to the first. The Arbegast Gang's career eventually ended upon the gallows, but I doubt it shall trouble my conscience much.

The Adventure of the Last Casualty

The spring of 1889 had been an unpredictable one, and one late evening in April found the great detective, Sherlock Holmes, and me ensconced in our sitting room at 221B Baker Street while the wind lashed the rain violently across the windows and howled wildly within the chimney. Holmes, his lean, acetic features clearly delineated by the glow of a lamp, sat in his long blue dressing gown at his desk. He was occupied with several piles of newspapers, which he was clipping and indexing for his files. With Mary off accompanying Mrs Cecil Forrester on a trip to the seaside, I was sitting in the basket chair by the fireplace, smoking, and relishing this chance to visit Holmes and our old rooms. Suddenly, he looked up, and turned toward the window.

"A cab has just pulled up outside, Watson. Surely, it is a client. Only a dire emergency could bring someone to our doorstep in this weather."

Predictably, the bell began to ring, and within moments, our landlady, Mrs Hudson ushered an unusually tall, middle-aged man into our quarters. He stood dripping at attention, and though a complete stranger, he immediately extended a hand to Holmes.

"Mr Sherlock Holmes, I am sorry to disturb you on a night like this, but I have just read something very disturbing in the papers and wish to consult with you about it."

"Please come in, Colonel. I have no doubt that only the utmost emergency could have compelled you to leave your home in Belgravia in such a storm. This is my friend and colleague, Dr Watson. You may rely on his discretion. Thank you, Mrs Hudson," said Holmes, closing the door behind her as she left.

"Why, Mr Holmes, my name is Hunter, and I am indeed a retired Colonel, but how did you…"

"The military bearing is obvious, and the regulation length of hair and moustache, the handkerchief in your sleeve are all giveaways. I also note the obvious air of authority and the army insignia attached to your watch chain, Colonel. You are rather young for an officer but are wearing the old school tie, so I would assume you rose quickly through the ranks, like so many in the last war. A bit too young for a Brigadier, but a Colonel or Lieutenant Colonel would be a reasonable assumption. That you are from that rather fashionable district in the West End I was able to deduce from that white line across your trouser leg. There are many neighbourhoods in London where one can find those popular white stucco houses, but only in Belgravia are several of those houses being refaced. You apparently stepped in a puddle containing a high concentration of debris from the stucco, and it is very visible at the edges of the splash upon your trousers. The storm and lateness of the evening indicate that you were at home when you were reading the paper. But, please, let us take your coat and pour you some brandy. Then you can warm yourself by the fire while you tell us what is the matter."

While the Colonel made himself comfortable in an armchair before the fire, Holmes and I took our seats.

"Have either of you yet read of the death of General Asquith in the latest editions?"

"Yes, he was found shot late this afternoon at his home in Piccadilly," replied Holmes. "But please, Colonel, tell us the whole story as you have it."

"He was shot with my gun, Mr Holmes, though I have not seen it in eleven years and have no idea how it could have got there."

Holmes' keen, gray eyes glinted, and he leaned forward intently, resting his chin upon his clasped hands.

"Yes, I remember the gun being a distinctive one," said Holmes. "An Enfield service revolver, but nickel-plated with pearl grips and a hair trigger."

"And, I know with a fear bordering on certainty, the initials HLH engraved upon it—my initials."

"I do not recall that detail from the papers, Colonel," I said. "Surely, though rare, there are other revolvers meeting *that* description."

"I am afraid that would be too much of a coincidence, Dr Watson," he said and then paused. "I shall start at the beginning. The revolver was well known to the men of my regiment, Mr Holmes. I was always slightly embarrassed by the ostentatiousness of the thing, but it was a gift from my parents, and I felt bound to carry it.

"As you remarked earlier, that second war with the Afghans quickly elevated the rank of many a young man, and Sir Michael Asquith was one of them. Despite his late arrival, he had managed to decimate our ranks by engaging us in several lopsided skirmishes over pointless objectives. Even in battles where our army ultimately triumphed, he managed to wrest a defeat for our regiment. Maiwand was not the only disaster of that war's second phase."

"I understand how you feel," I commiserated. "My first, and indeed last, experience of battle was at that bloody massacre."

"Ah, I am sorry, Doctor. That was a horror my unit was spared. We were a crack regiment–the 3rd Wessex Rifles– battle-hardened and perfectly trained in manoeuvring around that rugged country. It would have been so much worse for us if we had not been...

"It was at the battle of Kandahar. In fact, it was in the morning on the way there that we had to contend with some fortified villages before the army could push forward. Asquith chose to advance through an orchard despite the overwhelming Ghazi artillery. Just as we began to march into the relentless barrage, a light cavalry unit that had been scouting drew up asking me to direct them to Asquith. They had found an approach that offered greater cover. As rank after rank was mowed down, I kept looking toward the rear to see if this new intelligence would result in wiser, less suicidal orders. That never happened, and I led my men into oblivion. We did manage to capture the town with the help of the Sikhs, but that final, bloody, bayonet charge ensured that we would not be taking part in any future fighting."

Having served in that terrible conflict, I waited silently until the Colonel resumed. Holmes followed my example.

"There was nothing left for us to do that day but minister to the wounded and bury the dead. General Asquith had the gall to descend among us with many triumphant and congratulatory shouts. When he came over to congratulate me, I finally lost control of my temper.

"'Dozens of my best men blown to bits for no reason, and you think that cause for celebration!' I railed. 'Dozens of men who, had you been able to control your worst impulses and make your first intelligent tactical decision, would have survived to see this small victory, rather than eternity! It should be you, Asquith, lying in the dirt, instead of them!'

"It was at this point, to my shame, that I became completely insubordinate and pointed my revolver at the General's head. Though I think he was motivated by fear more than anything else, to his credit, he did not order me shot on the spot.

"'He then said, 'Given what you have just gone through and the timing, I will confine myself to ordering you to drop that gun this instant, or by God, in a few weeks time, you will be the last casualty of this war!'

"He was right. My anger was ultimately impotent and would never bring back those men or alleviate the horror of it all. I lowered the gun, humiliated, and waited for the hammer to fall, but it never did. The regiment, every man of which had just witnessed my shame, gathered around me, and I was led back to the medical tent. When I awoke late that night, I went for a walk outside the village, and becoming infuriated about the whole incident yet again, I threw the gun away and left it in the dust and the offal of Afghanistan. I have not seen it since.

"Shortly after the war ended I mustered out and came into a rather large inheritance after losing my parents and older brother to influenza. I hated Asquith, but things could have turned out much worse for me if he had behaved differently that day. But you can see that, if it is my gun that was found lying beside the General, I shall probably be considered a suspect."

Holmes lifted his head from his chest and looked languidly over his steepled finger tips, "And quite a good one. Did anyone see you throw away the gun?"

"Not that I know of, but if it has made its way back to England, someone must have and retrieved it."

"Is there anything else of note in the newspaper article, Watson?"

I quickly reread the brief article and noted points of possible interest.

"There is not much to go on. The body was found at 4:30 p.m. by the General's butler. The cause of death was a gunshot wound presumably fired by the unusual Enfield revolver that was lying by the body. Inspector Bradstreet is in charge of the investigation."

"Given how late the murder occurred, I am impressed the reporter even managed to get it into the late edition. Where were you at around that time, Colonel?"

"I had wanted to get in a short walk before the rain began, and was strolling around the neighbourhood."

"I don't suppose anyone can vouch for your whereabouts?"

"No, I am afraid not."

"Do you know of anyone who might wish the General harm?"

"I am sorry, Mr Holmes, but that miserable day in 1880 was the last time I saw the man. We do not travel in the same circles."

"Very well. If you do not object, I think it would be best for you to accompany us to the scene of the crime, Colonel, and make a statement to the police. They will almost certainly want to detain you, but it will be better for you to make all the facts known at the outset."

Donning our overcoats, we marched out into the roaring gale. In a short time, our cab deposited us at the General's white brick townhouse in Piccadilly. The bobby at the entrance nodded to Holmes from under his dripping umbrella, opened the door for us, and called out to those inside to let them know we had arrived. The tall, stout form of Bradstreet, in bowler and Mackintosh, emerged from one of the rooms off the long entrance hall, and he smiled warmly beneath his well-groomed moustache.

"Good evening Mr Holmes and Dr Watson. I do believe this is a new personal best for you, arriving with our chief suspect before we have even finished dusting for fingerprints."

"Always a pleasure, Bradstreet. I take it, then, you have learned the provenance of the revolver?"

"Indeed we have, gentlemen. The butler, a Mr Sorrell, has served with the General since the war and knows Colonel Hunter."

"The Colonel, suspecting that it was his gun that was found here, has retained me as a consultant."

"I admit that it is my gun, Inspector, but I swear I have not seen it since the war ended."

"Nevertheless, we will need to take a statement from you at the station, sir."

With that, Bradstreet waved to a young sergeant and gave him instructions to take charge of the Colonel. He then led Holmes and me into what turned out to be the General's study, which the General still occupied.

"General Asquith, gentlemen," announced Bradstreet as he waved his hand toward a body occupying a corner of the study. Nestled among the book-lined shelves along the walls, massive stone mantel, and occasional aspidistra, stood a large mahogany desk, leather couch, and several armchairs, all neatly arranged. The general, a bald, short, pudgy man in evening dress was still seated in his chair and slumped over the desk. A sizable exit wound in his back was visible from where we stood in the entrance.

"Clearly there was no struggle," said Holmes as he took out a magnifying glass and began his customary, minute examination of the scene much to the bemusement of those few policemen not familiar with his methods. Bradstreet, watching Holmes crawl along the carpet, took it all in stride and approached the body with me.

"One shot to the heart fired at close range from that revolver, I think you'll find, Dr Watson."

"A crack shot, indeed. The size of the entrance and exit wounds definitely correspond to a .476 calibre round. That it continued unimpeded through the back of the chair and into that shelf would further indicate it was fired from the Enfield," I noted as I continued to examine the corpse. "I would put the time of death at roughly 4:30, Holmes."

At that point Holmes had climbed halfway out of one of the two windows in the study.

"Was this window open when you arrived, Bradstreet?"

"It was open when Mr Sorrell entered the room and found the body. We are assuming the murderer escaped through it."

"And these wool fibres on the ledge lend credence to your assumption. The rain has washed away any chance of our following the murderer, but look here! There are a few tracks remaining directly below the window and in this flower bed. The shoe size is indeed the same as the Colonel's and the stride indicates a height of six feet five inches, which also matches the Colonel."

Holmes heaved himself back into the room and closed the window.

"The physical record of the crime gives us very little to go on. While the murderer's height and shoe size are somewhat remarkable, his wardrobe was not. I imagine most men in the General's circle own a dark wool suit and black brogue shoes. Even the two cigars in the ashtray are from that box on the General's desk. I should like to speak to Mr Sorrell, please, Bradstreet."

With this, we followed Inspector Bradstreet back out into the main hall, and were introduced to the General's manservant, who, though also of staunch military bearing, was clearly shaken. Bradstreet then led the three of us into the drawing room on the other side of the hall, and we congregated before the fire.

"Mr Sorrell, how long have you been in the General's employ?"

"I was part of his staff during the war, Mr Holmes, and shortly after he retired, he approached me to come and work for him here. I've known the man for almost fifteen years."

"Can you please recall the events of this afternoon, leading up to your finding the General had been shot?"

"Yes, sir. I was working in the kitchen and talking to the cook, when I heard the front door open. As I came into the hall, I only just had a glimpse of the General guiding the Colonel into the study. He then thanked me, but told me he did not need anything. He was polite enough, as he always was, but I could tell he was upset about something. An hour later, I heard what I was certain was a shot. Lord knows I've heard enough of them. I rushed into the hall and saw that the study door was still closed. I ran over to it and knocked to ask the General if he had heard it, too. When there was no answer...no sound, I had a bad feeling and tried the knob. It was locked, so I ran back to my room to get a spare key. He is still sitting there, just as I found him."

"Are you absolutely certain it was the Colonel you saw entering the study with him?"

"Well...not completely. I only saw the man from behind, but I know few men who are that tall and seeing that gun made me almost certain it was the Colonel. The last time I saw that particular revolver was when the Colonel was pointing it at the General's head at Kandahar. He should have been shot for that. He had always been a hothead. Thought he knew better than his commanders. He was lucky the General was such a patient man.

After all, who among us knew for certain that the approach those cavalrymen suggested wouldn't have wasted precious time. He certainly wasn't to know."

"Did the General have any other friends or associates that resembled the Colonel?"

"You know, he did at that. His old chum, Mr Merrison, is about the same height and build. He hasn't been round in quite some time, though. Works for the government over in Whitehall. They would often meet at either the Diogenes or Guards Clubs. But, like I said, the General and Mr Merrison are close friends, and the General's disposition when I saw him in the hall did not appear at all friendly to me"

"Thank you, Mr Sorrell. I have no further questions," said Holmes, and with a nod from Inspector Bradstreet, the butler left the room.

"You know, Holmes," I said, "I must admit I am starting to have my doubts about the Colonel."

"Yes," agreed Bradstreet. "A man fitting his description was with the General when the shot was fired by a gun he owned or owns. According to what I have heard from Sorrell, he seems to have a pretty good motive, as well."

"The way he described the General to us also seems to be not entirely reliable," I added.

"But why wait five years to enact his revenge?" asked Holmes. "It is one thing to serve the dish of revenge cold, but to wait that long seems positively lackadaisical. And if he did do it, why would he deliberately bring attention to himself by leaving the gun behind and then bringing me into the matter?"

He paused briefly, lighting a cigarette while he concentrated.

"No, I think I shall proceed on the assumption that his story about the gun is true."

"But then how did this fantastic gun make its way here from so many miles away and so many years ago?"

"You make it sound like the gambit of a sensational novel, Watson. Surely, we can draw a relatively straight line connecting the two points? Think back to The Colonel's story."

"Right, I suppose it could have been picked up by a soldier on the field that saw him throw it."

"Yes, but how many of them figure into our current drama?"

"Well, since we have no idea who the murderer is, anyone from the regiment could be the culprit, but...I must admit, it is probably more likely that the General picked up the pistol and brought it home with him."

"Excellent, Watson. You progress."

"Very well, but that still brings us no closer to identifying the murderer, unless you are going to tell me the General did that, as well."

"Mr Sorrell said he had not seen that gun since the war," interjected Bradstreet. "Surely he would have seen it at some point if the General had taken possession of it."

"That is a remarkably astute observation, Bradstreet, and it does introduce a degree of uncertainty. So we are agreed that, if the Colonel is to be believed, either the General had the gun, and for some reason, Mr Sorrell never saw it, or someone else from the regiment committed this murder. Or, even that someone from the regiment retrieved it and disposed of it in such a way that it made its way into the hands of our killer coincidentally, but the odds of such an event are so slim that it would be almost supernatural."

"The motive could be the same," I suggested. "And if it is a soldier taking revenge upon his former commanding officers, using the Colonel's gun would effectively kill two birds with one stone."

Holmes took a few thoughtful drags before concluding, "I must admit, that is a possibility, but let us not forget Merrison, our man from the Ministry. I propose we divide our labours and follow three lines of enquiry. Bradstreet, what if you investigate whether any soldiers from the Colonel's regiment have recently been released or escaped from prison? Watson, would you be able to get away from your practice long enough to do the same for asylums and sanitariums? I shall look into the General's friend, Merrison, and any other leads that may present themselves."

Having assented to this plan, Holmes and I departed for Baker Street. The next day, I began the extremely dreary task of contacting my fellow medical professionals at institutions from Broadmoor to Bedlam. Bradstreet, who had taken Holmes' advice and allowed the Colonel to return home with a promise not to leave the city, stopped by periodically while I awaited responses to tell me he was progressing just as abysmally. Though, I suppose it was reassuring to confirm the strong moral fibre of our British servicemen. Of Holmes there was no sight for the next several days. When he did return to our quarters, he did so long after I had retired and was up and gone the next morning before either Mrs Hudson or I had awakened. It was after dinner on the Wednesday of the week following our taking the Colonel's case, as I sat reading the paper, that Holmes burst into our sitting-room.

"Ah, Watson, you are here. It is good to see you after so many days."

"Welcome home, Holmes. Mrs. Hudson has left a cold collation on the sideboard if you are hungry. I take it you have a lead in the case?"

"Elementary," he said, as he eschewed the sideboard for his oily clay pipe on the mantel. "Merrison is our man, and I intend to beard him in his den this very evening. Bradstreet and Mycroft will be joining us shortly."

"Your brother, Mycroft? However did you persuade him to leave Whitehall or the Diogenes Club and why?"

"I thought it would be good to have him along given his contacts within the government and club membership. It turns out he does, indeed, know Merrison."

As I said that, the bell jangled, and we heard the familiar tread of Inspector Bradstreet upon the stairs.

"Hello, Holmes. Dr Watson," he said as he entered. "Ah, I see you have been kind enough to provide dinner. I haven't had a chance to have a bite since tea. Infernal departmental audit. What's this about you having a lead in the Asquith murder?"

Holmes wandered over to our table and beckoned for us to join him.

"As I was just telling Watson, since Mr Sorrell mentioned that Merrison worked in Whitehall, I thought first to get some background from my brother, Mycroft."

"He works in Whitehall, too, if I remember correctly."

"Yes, he audits the books for some Governmental departments, but he is well-connected. He was bound to know something of Merrison. According to Mycroft, Edward Merrison joined the Home Office a few years ago and holds a very senior position on the General Staff. Mycroft then had his secretary retrieve Merrison's address in Pall Mall for me.

"By ducking, at intervals, into the various boltholes I maintain around the city, I donned a variety of simple disguises while I was staking out his modest, red brick townhome. Lingering nonchalantly on the sidewalk opposite the house, I had my first sight of him as he returned that very evening, the day after General Asquith was murdered. His height, as you can imagine, gave him away immediately, and from a distance, if seen from behind and in poor light, he could be mistaken for the Colonel, though Merrison's hair is darker and he is clean-shaven. His build and bearing are also similar to Hunter's, which befits a former officer."

Holmes paused to repack his pipe with shag and after lighting it, continued.

"From this point, for several days, I followed him wherever he went. To his office in Whitehall, to his clubs in Pall Mall and Mayfair, to his stockbroker, and his bank. By Friday evening, I was beginning to consider abandoning this particular line of enquiry for there was nothing in Merrison's movements to suggest that he was involved in any criminal or even mildly inappropriate activity. Just as I was getting ready to call off the chase and return to Baker Street, he finally did something slightly unusual. It was well after sunset and the lamps had all been lit, so I had secreted myself in a narrow alley between two large townhomes. Across the street, in an upstairs window I had determined was Merrison's bedroom, a strange light appeared. Someone had lit a lamp with a peculiar red shade and moved it very close to the open window."

Holmes' gray eyes blazed as he recalled the thrill of this first possible clue. He took a long drag from his pipe and resumed his story.

"After about a half an hour, I became aware of another person nearby who was also interested in that red light. I retreated further into the alley as another man, the only passerby on my side of the street, slowed his pace slightly and glanced upward at that window a few times before resuming his former pace. He was heavyset, and his dour countenance was familiar to me. It was none other than Fedorin, a Russian diplomat that I and many others within the government have long suspected of being involved in espionage.

"Within another half an hour Merrison emerged from his house carrying a brown leather briefcase and began walking toward St James's Square. I followed him into Piccadilly and to his destination, the Criterion Restaurant. I discreetly took a seat at the bar, from which I was able to observe Merrison reflected in a mirror. Before long, who should also appear but Fedorin, who happened to be carrying an identical briefcase."

"Holmes, I think I am beginning to see, however vaguely," I said.

Holmes glanced at the clock and then leaned back and steepled his fingers.

"Unfortunately, at that stage, that was how I saw the affair, as well, but I had my lead. The next day, I spoke to Mycroft–who should be here any minute–and obtained the guidance and authority I needed. During the day, while Merrison was at work, he was closely observed by various coworkers who had been instructed by some of Mycroft's contacts. That left me free to visit his bank, stockbroker, and his clubs. Though reluctant at first, the imprimatur of the Foreign Office made the clerks at the bank and the brokerage more cooperative. Merrison, to use the vernacular, was skint. He had recently made some devastatingly poor investments in Central America, and his debts had been threatening to overwhelm him. But then, within the last few weeks, he had made a series of substantial cash deposits.

"Next, as a long-standing member of the Diogenes Club, Mycroft was able to prevail upon the livery. I spoke to one of the doormen, Mr Standing, who noticed the General and Merrison arguing as they departed the club on the evening of the murder. He did not catch the whole thing, but said there was an odd word that kept coming up. A Russian sounding word."

At that moment, the bell began to peel, and we heard an especially heavy tread upon the stairs. I opened the door to admit Holmes' brother, the enigmatic Mycroft. The family resemblance was unmistakable with the only significant difference in appearance between the two men being their weight. Mycroft's frame was as corpulent and flabby as Holmes' was lean and athletic.

"Dr Watson, so good to see you again. Good evening Inspector Bradstreet. Sherlock," he said as his drowsy looking eyes alighted upon each of us in turn.

"Welcome, Mycroft. I was just filling in Watson and Bradstreet."

"I should have thought with your penchant for drama, you would have kept that for the end, as you customarily do," Mycroft said with a slight smirk as he lowered his more than substantial bulk into one of our armchairs.

"I am sure there are surprises yet in store for all of us, brother mine. To continue, after establishing the facts I just related to you regarding Merrison, I returned to Whitehall to work out a plan with Mycroft. I then resumed my surveillance with some gentlemen generously supplied by one of my brother's colleagues. We awaited another signal from the red lamp, and tonight we have received it. I trust that a similar meeting occurred while I was talking with Watson and Bradstreet?"

"It has, indeed, Sherlock. Merrison and Fedorin are at the Criterion as we speak."

"Then we should probably depart for Pall Mall. You will want to bring your revolver, Watson. Merrison is reportedly fond of guns"

"We can take my carriage, Sherlock, and Bradstreet can follow us in his. You did get that warrant I arranged for you, Bradstreet?"

"Yes, I have it here, Mr Holmes."

The night was warm and humid, threatening more rain as we made our way to Pall Mall. We had soon pulled up to the red brick townhome and alighted with Bradstreet leading our party to Merrison's blue-painted door, warrant in hand. Bradstreet grabbed the brass ring and three loud knocks resounded in the night. Within a few moments, a shape could be discerned at the windows, and every single one of us tensed visibly as the door began to open. But it was only Merrison's manservant, a kind looking man of late middle-age, who was probably younger than he looked.

"I am Inspector Bradstreet of Scotland Yard. My colleagues and I need to have a word with Edward Merrison."

"I am sorry, Inspector, sir, but Mr Merrison has gone out."

"He has not yet returned from the restaurant?" asked Holmes.

"No, sir, but how did you..."

"Then we shall wait for him inside, please. I have a warrant here if you would like to inspect it."

"No, Inspector. Please, do come through."

We filed along into the long and narrow hall.

"Would you gentlemen like to sit down? What is this all about?"

"I thank you, sir, but I am going to need to ask you to please retire to the kitchen. We are on urgent government business, and what we have to say is strictly for Mr Merrison's ears only," said Sherlock Holmes softly. "Surely you understand," he said as he motioned the butler down the hall. After he had disappeared into the back of the house, Holmes turned back to us.

"Aha!" he exclaimed as he pointed toward a room to the left of the entrance whose door was standing open. It was obviously meant to be a study, but there were several regions of the tobacco-coloured walls that had been cleared of shelves so that rifles and muskets could hang in their place.

Holmes' eager, hawk-like features were alight as he darted swiftly through the doorway.

"If I am very lucky, there will just be enough time," he said as we followed him into the room.

Not only were there firearms of all sorts upon the wall–everything from flintlocks to matchlocks and some with the most exquisite carvings and engravings–but there were also two display cases for various pistols. Holmes, like a great bird of prey swooped down upon the first of these, his gray eyes blazing. The pistols, too, were quite remarkable–derringers, double-barrels, even an old pepperbox. Holmes clicked his tongue in disappointment before lighting upon the second case by the opposite wall. A smile spread across his face.

"Eureka," he said softly.

Almost as if on cue, Mycroft Holmes hissed for us to be quiet and pointed toward the hall. As if of one mind, we all drew further into the study and waited as the front door opened.

"Hello, Finley, I'm back," said a voice as it approached the doorway to the study. "If you could please...Oh, who are you?"

"Mr Edward Merrison, I am Sherlock Holmes, and I can see that you have already recognized my brother, Mycroft. Allow me to also introduce my friends and colleagues, Dr Watson and Inspector Bradstreet of the Yard."

I could see Merrison recomposing and steeling himself for what he had already assumed was going to be a confrontation.

"I would be pleased to make the acquaintance of you gentleman at any other time, but I am afraid my servant, Finley, erred when he admitted you. I have had a very trying day and have business yet to attend to. I am afraid that I must respectfully ask you to leave. Perhaps we can talk tomorrow at a more civil hour."

"It won't do, Merrison," said Mycroft languidly. "As you have already guessed, I am here representing your employer. We know exactly how busy you are and with what. We shall not be put off."

Merrison was sweating more profusely than was justified by the sultry air, and his face grew pale.

"Indeed, my brother and I would like to know all about your recent dinner companion," said Holmes.

"Please, Mr Holmes, you do not understand," said Merrison to Mycroft. "When Fedorin approached me, I saw an opportunity to deceive him, exercise my initiative."

"And enhance your bank account," interjected Sherlock Holmes. "It is hard to believe your good friend, General Asquith, would have taken such issue with your heroic attempt at counter-espionage. I think it is more reasonable to conclude he was threatening to expose your treachery, and for that, you killed him."

"Kill Asquith? Isn't that disgruntled Colonel he hated under suspicion for that?"

"He was," Sherlock Holmes said, smiling out of the corner of his mouth at Bradstreet, "briefly. It was the Colonel's gun that killed him, after all. There is no denying that. But, it seemed so odd that the Colonel would have waited so long to have concluded his quarrel with the Colonel, and even stranger that he would have left a murder weapon so thoroughly associated with himself behind at the scene. No, the Colonel threw that revolver into the dust of Afghanistan just as he claimed, and the General, having seen him, picked it up. Whether to return it to him or keep it for himself, we shall never know. The General did, however, give it away in short order. He gave it away to a comrade who had an interest in such rare firearms, and you kept it right here until you found a particular purpose for it."

"But what are you talking about? That's just an ordinary Enfield revolver in that case."

"It is now. Watson, Bradstreet, if you could step over toward the door there. I would rather Mr Merrison stay with us for a while. Mycroft, please take a look at this case with Merrison and I. It contains more modern legendary firearms, such as this pearl-handled Peacemaker and that Colt Navy, but…"

"It also rather incongruously contains a battered, old Enfield in this corner. There is nothing remotely interesting about it, which suggests a placeholder," observed Mycroft.

"A place of honour originally held by Colonel Hunter's Enfield, which the General gave to Merrison. You can see the outline in the felt of the engraving on that gun's nickel plating, even just make out the initials. I believe that just about does it, eh, Bradstreet? A man fitting Merrison's description was observed at the scene, the murder weapon belonged to him–and could even conveniently deflect attention to a possible suspect– and he had an excellent motive for killing his old friend."

"I must hand it to you, Holmes. Very neat," said Bradstreet.

"Mr Holmes, sir, please," Merrison entreated Mycroft Holmes. "I can still be of use, pass off disinformation to Fedorin and the rest."

"Thank you, Mr Merrison, but thanks to my brother, you have already performed the only counterintelligence duty we shall ever need of you. I imagine those documents you provided Fedorin this evening will confuse the Russians for some years to come."

"I'm not sorry to say it seems likely that, thanks to Mr Holmes, you shall swing for at least one of these crimes. You're under arrest, Merrison," said Bradstreet as he placed Merrison in handcuffs and escorted him to the car.

"It is so hard to imagine betraying one's country so easily after having benefited so much from it," I said, glancing around at all of the treasures on the walls.

"Not to mention turning on a close personal friend," added Sherlock Holmes.

"It is probably best not to dwell on it too deeply," replied Mycroft, "To be brutally honest, without people like him, the work of many of my colleagues would not be at all possible."

The Adventure of Mr Abcdarius

It is reassuring to think back on the familiar sitting room at 221B Baker St where I once sat at my desk going over my notes from our various adventures while Sherlock Holmes played his violin before a roaring fire. I have begun many of my stories describing those cosy surroundings before the two of us were once again inevitably plunged into mystery and sometimes danger. But it has been quite some time since I last resided at that address, and the beginning of this particular case was as far from cosy and familiar as any could possibly get. It was on a soggy, late morning in April, 1903 when, following a loud banging on the door of my Queen Anne Street practice, a shabbily dressed and dripping young urchin loudly bounded into my office bearing a message from Holmes himself:

"I'm off to meet a potential client at the Lunatic Asylum at Hurndle and may need medical advice. If convenient, meet me there. If inconvenient, come all the same."

I recall sighing grumpily, but, of course, he knew that there was no chance that I would pass up joining him at that most unlikely of locations. I quickly despatched the boy to the telegraph office with a few quick messages to that day's remaining patients. At this point in my professional life, my practice was not inconsiderable, and dropping everything to join Holmes in another adventure was anything but convenient. But meeting Holmes at an asylum was far more tempting than ministering to seasonal allergies, and I followed the young man out the door and hailed a hansom. Having promised the cabbie a sovereign if he would not spare the horse, we barrelled along through London and the rain to the western outskirts of the city, the driver seemingly able by some magical trick of the trade to see through the fog that was descending. Even at speed, it was over an hour before we arrived in Ealing and drew up before the imposingly gated, brick archway of the entrance to the asylum grounds. The lowering sky had darkened significantly since I had set out, and thunder was beginning to rumble. A gatekeeper in livery opened the heavy, creaking gate for us, and the cab proceeded to the roundabout of Hurndle's palatial courtyard. The place more accurately resembled a fortress than a palace, though, and the gray walls of the west wing loomed over us on our left as we drove in a semicircle toward the long central building that connected that wing with the east one. Despite the well-tended flowers and statuary in the centre of the roundabout, the gloom that hung over the yard was pervasive, and it was not just a chill breeze that caused me to shiver. The driver pulled before the entrance of the central building, and I disembarked. Noticing that mine was the only cab there, I asked the poor man to find shelter and wait. I then rushed inside to get out of the rain, noting a Masonic compass and square symbol chiselled into the granite keystone over my head. In the large hall, even the white walls and polished black linoleum floor managed to look dreary as the light from all of the windows diminished. I immediately spotted Holmes talking to a doctor in a white laboratory smock while other men in smocks and nurses in uniform bustled about the place.

"Ah, Watson! You've made exceptional time for once. Allow me to introduce you to Dr Quentin Hislop. He has recently admitted a patient who desires to speak with us."

"Yes, a Mr Harris Dawes," confirmed the Doctor. "A couple of bobbies dragged him in here a few hours ago. He was screaming about some foreign chap and a curse. Calmed down after being lightly sedated and asked to speak to Mr Holmes while we were removing the restraints. It put his mind more at ease when I agreed to ring you. It's been a rather crowded morning, so I'll take you to him directly."

We quickly set out for what appeared to be the east wing, passing a large oak registration desk in the main hall along the way. As we turned to the right and passed through two large wooden double-doors, we entered a long hall with rooms on either side. The hissing of the gaslights became more audible as the sound of the rain was muted by the lack of windows.

"You'll appreciate, Dr Watson, that we take a humanistic approach to our patients," said Hislop. "Despite the dramatic weather, there are no horrors here. Just people who are ill and receiving treatment. If the weather were better, you'd see more of them about. The flowers you no doubt saw in the roundabout—selected, planted, and maintained by our patients. See the common room there? Painting, knitting, and games to play."

Indeed, in the large room were about fifteen patients all engaged in one activity or another. All were quiet, even if some of them had an affect that was obviously not entirely conventional. There were only a few patients in the hallway, and one woman passed close to me while walking in the opposite direction, gazing vacantly and muttering, "Here he comes, the Magic Man," while twirling her hair with one finger. I thought at the time that hers was a mystery that would be worth solving as she padded past us in her slippers. Dr Hislop motioned to what looked like a burly attendant who immediately joined us.

"With me, Mr Haines. Going to visit Dawes in A21. He seemed placid enough last I saw him, but you never know. Might become frantic again."

In room A21, a clean-shaven, portly, middle-aged man sat slumped on the bed along the wall opposite the door. It was dark, but the low illumination of the gas and the occasional flash of lightning illuminated him well enough for us to see that his charcoal suit, though rumpled with a tear at the right shoulder, was clearly well-made. What hair he still possessed was dishevelled. Behind him, the rain was streaming down the outside of the long, narrow windows with a racket that almost drowned out the thunder.

"How are you holding up, old man? Not letting this frightful weather get to you, I hope." asked Hislop, checking Dawes' temperature and pulse with his hand. "This is Mr Sherlock Holmes and Dr Watson, as you requested. Do you feel up to visiting with them?"

"Yes, Dr Hislop, upon my life, there are no other people I'd rather see right now, for I am certain you're the only ones who can possibly help me. Mr Holmes and Dr Watson, I am Mr Harris Dawes, the owner of Dawes' Curious Corner in Soho and Adeptus Exemptus and Imperator of the Esoteric Society of the Roseate Morn. It is due to the latter occupation that my life is now in danger. Perhaps you've heard of our Society?"

114

"Unless your organisation is a criminal enterprise, it would be unlikely," Holmes replied laconically, pulling a wooden chair over to the bed and settling into it. "Pray, tell your story from the beginning and omit nothing, no matter how unusual."

As Dawes began his unsettling narrative, I found another small chair and sat down to take notes. Dr Hislop and the orderly remained standing and seemed to become less impatient and the narrative progressed. The rain and thunder continued their row outside.

"We are an organisation devoted to the study of Magick. That is 'Magick' with a capital 'M', a 'c', and a 'k', *true* magic, the mystical wisdom of the ancients. We are not a large organisation but do include a few prominent writers and artists among our members. One member has recently made himself particularly notorious, the fantastically named Mr Abcdarius. And, no, no one knows his real name. He joined last year after returning to England from a stint abroad. He is believed to be independently wealthy, and some have even said he can turn metal into gold. He has no occupation other than the study of Magick, though I've learned his hobbies also include such pursuits as smoking hashish, feuding with other Society members, and adultery. Surely, you have heard his name mentioned?"

"Yes, I remember he was questioned after the suicide of General Maddox of the Suffolk Regiment a few months ago. Styles himself "the wickedest man in London", but he hardly merits the title in my opinion. I don't believe he was found to have had anything to do with the death."

"No, but he did call on the General, directly after which the man shot himself."

"Correlation but not necessarily causation," stated Holmes.

"But the thing is, Mr Holmes, we had a suicide in our own ranks recently. After a meeting a several weeks ago, a few of us went down to our local pub, The Wrong Answer. Reginald Curry, a socialite who has been a member for a few years, lived a block away from me and accompanied me on my walk home when we departed. Apropos of nothing, he turned to me and blurted, 'But what about old Abcdarius?' and then fell silent. It was as if he had read my mind, for a recent scandal had come to my attention. He could not have known that, though, as I had not mentioned it to any of the members yet. I asked him what it was about Abcdarius that he wanted to talk about, but he grew agitated and said he should not have brought him up. I tried pressing him, but he would say nothing more. The next morning, his valet found him in his tub. He had slit open the veins in both forearms."

"Most remarkable. This scandal, did it involve blackmail by any chance?" asked Holmes as the lightning flashed.

"I would not put it past the man, but no. That is a different matter and leads us directly to my predicament."

The thunder boomed loudly as Holmes nodded and leaned back as far as the small wooden chair would permit, eyelids beginning to droop.

"From the beginning, Abcdarius has had a curious hold on one of our members, Silas Johns. Johns was fortunate enough to have been born both noble *and* exceedingly wealthy. I always worried that he had turned to Magick, because like so many of that ilk, money was not enough for him. It has recently come to my attention that the two men have been performing some of the vilest and most dangerous rites known to us. These are summonings *from which* our group should be responsible for protecting the world. They also involve rituals that are…immoral…and, in fact, illegal. I convened the Society a few weeks ago without the villains, and we voted unanimously to expel them. Both were notified of this the next day and assured that we would turn our attention to thwarting any further summonings of such a kind. An announcement was also printed in *The Telegraph*.

I mentioned that I have a small shop in Soho and was there late on Friday night, going over the accounts after the shop had closed. Only myself and William Pitt, the Elder, my macaw and constant coworker were in the building. From the back office, where I was working, I suddenly heard Billy squawk loudly and then exclaim, 'Harris Dawes! Harris Dawes! The Devil's come for you!'"

Lightning tore the sky as if on cue and brightly illuminated a broad grin on Holmes' otherwise tranquil face.

"I take it that is not a phrase you taught your macaw?" he asked.

"No, Mr Holmes. It is assuredly not. I sat bolt upright when I heard it and could feel the hairs on the back of my neck standing on end. I listened, but the shop had become almost completely silent once again. I picked up the oil lamp and cautiously walked out into the shop itself. It was quite dark. The only illumination aside from my lamp came from the gas lamps outside the front window. The display counter is just outside the office door, and I walked behind it to check on Billy, who was in his cage just behind the register. He immediately greeted me with a 'Hallo, Harry! Give us a kiss!', which is his usual salutation. I satisfied myself that he was alright and noticed a business card lying on the counter that I am certain was not there before. I picked it up and…Well, here it is."

He handed the card to Holmes who then handed it to me. All that was printed on it was this:

Mr Abcdarius
The Devil in the Flesh

I read it aloud for the others and handed it back to Holmes, who gestured to Dawes to continue.

"On the back was printed: 'Reconsider your actions or else.' Oh, I know–it's not there now. The writing disappeared at some point before the next morning. I placed the card in my pocket and glanced around the shop once more. There was no one else there. I placed a cloth over Billy's cage as I do every night before locking up so that the bird would go to sleep, and I went back into the office to get my coat and hat before leaving. On my way out, I placed the lamp on the counter and blew it out. As I made my way to the front door, I heard a weird rattling in the corner to my right. It was a rattling of bones, Mr Holmes! A skeleton I had purchased some time ago, turned its head to gaze at me. It was as if I was frozen in place. I could do nothing but stand there watching it as it slowly raised its right arm and extended its index finger to point directly at me. It then threw back its head and laughed demonically! I am not ashamed to say that I ran out the door in terror at that point without even checking to make sure the door had locked behind me. I ran the whole way to my home in St James with no regard for the startled looks all the passersby were giving me.

"I saw the most awful shapes in my study's fire that night before drifting off to sleep. For what felt like hours, I felt rooted in place like a snake that had been charmed. I dared not sleep in the dark. The next day, I forced myself to return to the shop and saw nothing unusual. I began to wonder if I had imagined any of the events from the prior night, and if I had, which ones. The card was still in my wallet so that much was real. While I was locking that horrid skeleton away in an upstairs storage room, I resolved to tell the other members of the Society about the events at our next meeting.

"The next day passed without incident, but this morning, I had yet another shock. As I was dressing before leaving for work, I walked over to the mirror that hangs over my dresser in my bedroom. As soon as I was standing before it, I no longer saw my own reflection. Mr Holmes, it was the face of Abcdarius looking out at me, staring right into me! As I jumped aside in fright, I once again saw my normal reflection, but I did not approach the accursed glass a second time. I hurriedly put on my coat and hat and ran outside. The walk to the shop calmed me down a bit, and I thought, since I was early, some breakfast would not go amiss. I stopped at a cafe and was seated at a small table for one. After the host had seated me, I noticed my table had no menu, but a voice that was familiar, but not immediately recognizable, said from behind me, "Here, you can have mine. I know what I'm having," and passed the menu over my shoulder to me. I muttered a thank you and began looking over it. It was then that I recognized the voice. It was Abcdarius! I swung around to look behind me, but he was nowhere to be seen. I thought for a moment and then began to closely examine the menu with shaking hands. And there it was, fluttering as if in a breeze, a thin paper slip with runic letters written on it, lying between two pages! On one of the pages was written, 'Two weeks are permitted', the words of which had already begun to disappear! I remember very little after that aside from hearing my own shrieks and seeing the restaurant spinning and somersaulting around me."

"Yes, the bobbies said you were lying on the ground yelling about a demon and laughing while a few good samaritans hovered over you trying to get you to calm down and making sure you didn't hurt yourself. One of them even caught the paper slip before it blew away and handed it to them. Here it is, Mr Holmes. Oh, sorry. It's hard to hold on to."

The slip suddenly glowed in his hand as lightning flashed outside.

"Thank you, Doctor. I take it, Mr Dawes, that you believe this to be some sort of curse?"

"Yes, without a doubt. If I cannot pass that slip of runes back to the one responsible for it, it is my death warrant. You have to help me do that, Mr Holmes! He resides at Lufford Hall in Hampstead! I'll give you anything if only you can save me from that accursed Devil!"

"Restrain yourself, Mr Dawes!" exclaimed the detective as the thunder roared again, and Dr Hislop approached the bed with a syringe. After the doctor had administered another dose of sedative, the detective continued.

"Of course I shall help you with this problem. You should know my rates are on a fixed scale and do not vary and that this agency stands flat-footed upon the ground. I do not believe in magic, and will ensure that this man, Abcdarius, is no threat to you. The first thing Dr Watson and I shall do will be to examine your home and shop and make sure they are safe for you. When we have accomplished that, I will contact Dr Hislop. Do you trust us to do so?"

"Oh, I do, Mr Holmes. I feel better already knowing that you are on my side."

"Very good. In the meantime, may I hold onto this card and the runes?"

"Please do, and find a way for me to get those ruins into his hands, Mr Holmes. By hook or by crook, I must get them into his hands."

With that, we left Harris Dawes to get some sleep. Dr Hislop said he intended to keep the man overnight to make sure he would be alright and despatched Haines for our cab. For his part, Holmes promised Dr Hislop he would send a telegraph later with an update. Then, after a few minutes, another liveried doorman appeared to tell us our cab was ready outside, and we departed for Dawes' home in St James.

"Quite an extraordinary tale. What do you make of it, Holmes?"

"I think our friend, Dawes, has a rather extraordinary imagination. Stage magic. You can count on all this being nothing more than that. Misdirection and suggestion. I'm sure we'll learn the tricks before the day is through, but this Abcdarius interests me. If he is a blackmailer, he must be new to the game or surely he would have come to my attention before. Yes, we may be able to curtail his criminal career before it even truly begins."

And with that he fell silent. The thunder had ceased, and the sky had begun to lighten by the time we arrived at Dawes' street. We got out of the cab and walked through a misty drizzle to the house, a small but neat, white brick townhouse. Dawes' butler opened the door in response to our knock and led us into a neat, whitewashed hall. He was a clean-shaven man in his fifties named Torrence and showed genuine concern when we apprised him of Dawes' current situation.

"Are there any other servants?" asked Holmes.

"Just the cook, my wife, Mr Holmes. As you can see, it is not a large house, and we leave in the evenings after dinner."

"Have you been in Dawes' bedroom today?"

"No, sir. I normally would have made the bed by now, but we're waiting for the laundry. It's late today. No doubt due to the weather. I figured I would change the linens upstairs after it arrives."

"Very good, I should like to examine it."

Torrence directed us to the room, and we climbed the stairs to the first floor. Dawes' room was in the front of the building and was modestly if somewhat garishly furnished.

"Ah, these yellow aesthetes with their decadence and their sunflowers as one notorious critic has put it," said Holmes as we regarded the colourful yellow bedclothes and strange paintings that adorned the walls. The dresser Dawes mentioned was along the same wall as the door and was a bit more pedestrian looking. I have to admit, I felt a small thrill as we both approached the mirror that hung over it, but it stubbornly refused to show us anything other than our own reflections. Holmes motioned for me to stand still and immediately dropped to the floor to look for footprints. He then closely examined the windows. Exiting the room, he entered the next small room beside it. This turned out to be some sort of mystical dressing room, with Dawes' various gowns, robes, capes, and headdresses hanging from hangers and assorted dummies.

"Ah, just here, Watson. See the square-toed footsteps leading into this corner and the line across the rug just there, where the edge of something like a mirror has been sitting. And this small window. Yes, the latch has been forced and there is a fire escape. Someone has definitely paid an unwelcome visit to our Mr Dawes and even stayed the night last night."

We then rushed back downstairs and walked into the first room in the hall which Dawes had turned into his study. While Holmes examined the fireplace, I wandered over to one of the many full bookshelves and noted some of the extraordinarily titled contents–*The Book of Eibon*, *The Rituals of the Goetia*, *Unaussprechlichen Kulten*, and *Liber Ivonis*. I wondered from where the human skull resting on his enormous walnut desk had come. I had almost resorted to looking over some of his atrocious paintings when Holmes stood back up.

"Nothing, but I suppose that is not entirely surprising. Who knows what kinds of horrors surroundings such as these could produce in so fanciful an imagination as Dawes'. I suppose further wonders await us at his shop."

The rain had completely stopped, and I requested some coffee for our brave cab driver. After he had finished the drink and cakes Mrs Torrence had brought him, we departed for Soho. Soon, we drew up before Dawes' Curious Corner and its large, grimy front window.

"You know, Holmes, I don't seem to recall your asking Dawes for his keys," I said as we approached the door.

"Yes, it's not often I get to employ my lockpicking skills anymore, but I like to keep a hand in."

It took him no longer to open the door with his implements than it would have taken me with a key. The bells overhead clanged loudly as we opened and closed the door, and an odd, gurgling voice called "Hallo! Hallo!" Holmes walked across the floor, went behind the counter, and then over to the cage. He raised the purple cloth from it, and a striking bird with blue, green, and yellow feathers began bobbing up and down excitedly on its perch.

"Hallo, Harry! Give us a kiss! Give us a kiss!"

"You probably thought your owner forgot about you in all the commotion," said Holmes quietly as he refilled the bird's dish with food and water he found under the counter.

"Daddy's little piggy!" exclaimed the bird as it eagerly devoured the seeds.

Holmes then looked all around the shop and waved for me to stop as I was about to light the gas.

"Notice that corner, Watson. That has to be the one where the skeleton resided. It's quite dark right now, and would have been completely obscured by shadow last night. It is suggestive, is it not? Please, go ahead and light the gas."

He walked back around the counter and over to the dark corner, which he examined minutely. He then knelt to the floor and grunted in frustration.

"There are what I assume to be the depressions in the floorboards made by the stand and skeleton. Unfortunately, Dawes is too fastidious a housekeeper and has not left enough dust to create any footprints. Still, there's more than enough room for two men to stand here or a man and a skeleton," he said. "But how did the intruder get in?"

Practically hidden behind all of the weird bric a brac, like a shelf full of shrunken heads, several dusty mirrors, even more dubious artwork and literature than we found in the house, was a narrow stairway. Holmes quickly ascended while I lit my pipe and perused a recent volume by AE Waite. When Holmes returned, he looked satisfied.

"There are two storage rooms containing even more of this rubbish, including the skeleton. One of the window latches has been forced. Better still, the rooms were quite dusty, and our intruder wore the same square-toed shoes he was wearing when he visited Dawes' house, and from both sets of prints, it's clear he favours his left foot." Grinning, he turned to me and said, "The game's afoot, Watson."

After turning out the lights and replacing William Pitt, the Elder's purple cloth, we exited the shop.

"Watson, could you arrange to join me in Baker Street tomorrow morning? I think things will progress quickly from here."

"Certainly, Holmes. I'll get a *locum* in and join you for breakfast."

"Good old Watson. Please take the hansom. I have further inquiries to make and won't be needing it."

I returned to the office to arrange for Anstruther to take over my practice for a few days, and more importantly, I next sought my wife, Juliet's, approval. Having secured both, the following morning found me in Baker Street, digging into the breakfast Mrs Hudson had provided while Holmes filled his briar pipe with tobacco from the Persian slipper.

"This man intrigues me, Watson. I spent the rest of the day doing research on Abcdarius and am none the wiser. He claims to be English, but he doesn't seem to have any ties to anyone in this country. There are certainly no other 'Abcdarii' in England. In fact, the earliest trace of him I was able to find was in a newspaper article on The Valley of the Kings. The journalist mentions a few of the people she encountered on her trip to the pyramids, one of whom was 'the improbably named English magician, Mr *Abecedarius*'. That's with two extra 'e's. Apparently his mononym is a legal one, for the deed to Lufford Hall in Somerset House bears only the name 'Abcdarius', and there is no mortgage on the property. Where did he get his money? Is he a criminal? Why hasn't he come to my attention? Perhaps he was blackmailing Maddox and Curry, but if he was, their secrets died with them."

"The Devil in the Flesh," I replied.

"Absurd. Those tricks are stage magic, the kind of which you would find in any second rate music hall act."

"So tell me, how was it all done?" I said, egging him on. I knew that when Sherlock Holmes was in a loquacious mood, it was best to take every advantage.

"You'll recall I found the same square-toed footprints at both the shop and the residence? It is obvious he cased both places well before the activities of the past few days. Let's begin with the shop. He had broken in earlier in the day, and knowing Dawes' habits, waited until dark. The cry of the macaw was merely ventriloquism. As for the disappearing writing on the card, and subsequently the menu, you've seen me create invisible ink on more than one occasion. After placing the card, he could have then retreated to that dark corner of the shop and, wearing all black, including a head covering, moved the skeleton without being detected. As for the house, I could find nothing unusual about the fireplace, but I imagine Dawes' imagination picked up where our amateur magician left off. Human beings have been seeing shapes in the fire since its discovery. The mirror trick could have been accomplished by replacing the original with a duplicate containing platinized glass. Look at it from one direction, the subject will see his reflection. From another, an image behind the glass. Again, our Abcdarius has money. He would have needed it to make a copy of the Dawes' mirror, but he did have a few weeks to have it constructed. On the other hand, maybe he's a carpenter, too, for all I've learned about him."

"That's an awful lot of work to force a retraction and reinstatement into the Society."

"But that would be currency to a man pretending to be well-versed in the dark arts. If he can convince others that he has supernatural powers, he can increase his influence and enhance his extortion efforts. I just don't understand how a person who professes to study magic, like Dawes, cannot see through these flimsy tricks."

"But he studies 'Magick' with a 'k'," I joked.

"Fair enough. I think it is time for us to meet this Abcdarius 'in the flesh', as it were. That will surely prove educational if nothing else."

The day was warm and bright, and another long cab ride conveyed us to Hampstead. Lufford Hall was an imposing, rose-coloured, brick manor on its own grounds at the edge of the Heath, whose three stories towered over us as we approached the large white doors of the front entrance from the neat, dirt lane that led up to it. After directing the cabbie to wait, Holmes and I approached the door, and he rang the bell. In a few moments, a sturdily-built, middle-aged butler with a pug nose greeted us at the door and had no sooner asked us our business when a man in a dark frock coat emerged from one of the rooms off the large entrance hall and hailed us.

"I say, are you here for the seance? You are a bit early, and I do not recognize you. Still, the more the merrier," he said smiling. He was on the chubby side and bore a smile on his cherubic face. The narrow fringe of hair around his bald pate was rather unusually brushed upwards and so were his unusually long eyebrows. He was clean-shaven aside from a small goatee. These last small details gave him an unusual look that was, aside from his good natured expression, somewhat devilish.

"Mr Abcdarius, I presume? My name is Sherlock Holmes, and I am a consulting detective. This is my friend and colleague, Dr Watson. We are here on behalf of my client, an acquaintance of yours by the name of Horace Dawes."

"Oh, Dawes, you say. I heard the old boy had taken ill. Does this visit have something to do with that? Please, Morten will take your hats and coats. If we could go into the parlour over here to talk. I apologise for having to divide my attention, but the seance guests will be here shortly, and I need to prepare."

Our footsteps clopped along the tiled floor as we passed through the large hall filled with plants and classical busts on stands, and I noticed Abcdarius walked with a slight limp. The parlour was quite dark and a round mahogany table surrounded by chairs dominated the centre of the room. Other chairs, tables, and a desk radiated out from this along the periphery. Lavender curtains kept out most of the light, and the gaslights hissed in the walls. Abcdarius sat behind his desk pulling some books and notebooks out of a drawer while talking to us.

"So how is old Dawes, Mr Holmes? He and I are members of the same club, so to speak. Please, take a seat."

Holmes regarded the round table for an instant and sat down in one of the chairs, while I claimed an armchair by one of the windows.

"Last I saw him, he was in a rather agitated state. He said it had something to do with this," said Holmes as he pulled the fluttering slip of paper with the runes on it from his coat pocket and held it up.

"Oh, dear. That's rather serious. Any idea how much time is allowed?"

"Two weeks from yesterday. I'm not sure exactly what that means as far as time of day."

"At midnight, next Tuesday. That is how that particular curse works. You did specify that you're borrowing the slip, I hope?"

"Does that matter?"

"Like most Magick, it comes down to the force of the will. If he intended to pass the curse along to you and you accepted the slip willingly, it is now you who will die in two weeks."

"That would explain why the man is still terrified. You would do me a great service if you would simply take it back," said Holmes, rising to his feet and stepping toward the desk.

Abcdarius rose quickly and raised both hands in the air.

"No thank you, Mr Holmes."

Holmes returned the slip to his pocket and sat back down.

"It won't do, sir. I will not allow you to continue to threaten Dawes."

"You suspect me?" asked Abcdarius, resuming his seat, as well.

"Size eight shoes with square toes. A slight limp caused by favouring the left leg. I observed where you waited for nightfall on the first floor of Dawes' shop and where you waited for daybreak with Dawes' mirror in his home. That was just the first day's work. What more will I discover if I continue to investigate you? I'm going to make this easy for you. Meet with me and Dawes, tell him you will cease your harassment, and take back the slip of paper from him. Surely, as a reasonable man…"

"But I am not a *reasonable* man, Holmes. Not a bit. Some things are harder to stop than to start. You would do well to drop it. I am the one whose reputation has been smeared. Yes, those other tricks were merely that, but what you have in your pocket is the *real* thing. You have no idea the power I've beheld during the Enochian Invocations or the Bornless Ritual. Hermes Trismegistus, John Dee, Karl von Eckartshausen, they were right. Real Magick is a third way between science and religion, and it is absolutely *real*," said Abcdarius leaning forward in his chair. As he spoke, I noticed that it was suddenly getting dark outside the window, and the wind was beginning to stir the tree branches.

"Magick is getting into communication with individuals who exist on a higher plane than ours. Mysticism is the raising of oneself to their level. This is absolutely possible, and *I* have accomplished it. In this house, we are surrounded by Magick. The very house itself, Lufford Hall, was built upon ley lines identified by Nicholas Hawkesmoor. Yes, sir, it would be best for you to drop it. What you are dealing with is beyond your comprehension and absolutely and inescapably fatal. If you would like to continue to negotiate, make Dawes see reason, retract his statement, and allow me back into the Society. Otherwise, God help you both."

With that the sky opened up and rain began lashing the house. It was as dark as night aside from the occasional flash of lightning. An older woman in an apron entered the room, and Holmes and I stood.

"It's all kicking off now. Would you and your friends like some refreshments? I have a kettle on and there's ice cream."

"No, Mother, I'm afraid my guests are getting ready to leave as soon as this storm passes."

"Very well. It's just a summer squall. I can hear the rain slowing down already."

"Mrs Abcdarius?" asked Holmes. The woman looked at him and nodded. "Thank you, but as your son said, I'm afraid we must take our leave.

"Mother, would you be good enough to show Mr Holmes and Dr Watson the door. I still have more to prepare. Good day, gentlemen."

By the time our cab reached the end of the drive, the rain had stopped, and the sky had begun to clear.

"The Devil in the Flesh," I commented again as we departed.

"Don't be foolish," grunted Holmes.

"I have to admit, Holmes, I'm starting to feel uneasy about this man."

"Stuff and nonsense. It is only a coincidence. We know this, because it is elementary. There is no such thing as magic, with a 'k' or without. As I said, this agency must always stand flat-footed upon the ground. No wizards, warlocks, or incubi need apply. Speaking of which, I should like to be a fly on the wall at his little seance. While I was sitting at his table, I unscrewed these from it," he said, holding up two brass hooks.

"And what are those?"

"Mediums attach chains from their waistcoats to them in order to make it look like the table is levitating. It's a tiny act of sabotage, but I couldn't resist it when I saw them. There will be two more hooks on the other side for an accomplice. If Abcdarius doesn't notice the problem until too late, that little piece of hocus pocus will result in his stooge clumsily wrenching up only his side of the table."

Having been brought back down to earth once more, we returned to Baker Street. I poured two glasses of scotch and soda and sat down in the basket chair while Holmes took his place in the easy chair. After we had lighted our pipes and smoked for a while, Holmes broke the silence.

"I had hoped to elicit some sort of reaction from 'Mother' while we were talking."

"Yes, she did not react when you addressed her as 'Mrs Abcdarius. I noticed that *and* his limp."

There was a ring at the door below and soon light footsteps were bounding up the seventeen steps to our sitting room. Holmes opened the door to receive a telegram from the panting young man and asked him to wait for him to compose a message of his own. After placing the message and some coins in the boy's hand, Holmes sent the lad on his way and resumed his seat.

"That was from Hislop. Dawes was released from the asylum earlier and is at home now. I asked the boy to deliver a message from me to Dawes asking for an audience tomorrow."

I departed for Queen Anne Street after I had emptied my glass and my pipe. As I walked down the stairs, I could hear Holmes plucking at his violin to tune it.

The following morning, I received a telegram from Holmes asking me to meet him for lunch in St James so that we could then pay the ailing man a visit. That afternoon found us once again in front of the neat, brick townhouse where we were greeted by Torrence. After taking our hats, he led us into the familiar, garishly decorated study and told us that Dawes would be down momentarily. This time, a particular painting I had not noticed before caught my attention. It vividly depicted a group of scantily clad people dancing around a circle of bright light in a field. Surrounding them were standing stones that seemed to be transforming into grotesque, anthropomorphic figures.

"More decadence and yellow degradation, eh, old friend?" asked Holmes, grinning.

"It is more like some sort of rural horror."

"Remarkable isn't it?" said Dawes, as he entered the drawing room. His voice was much steadier, though he was still quite pale and dressed in a burgundy dressing gown. "I found it in an antiques stall in Avebury. No idea who painted it. Please take a seat and tell me about what you have found out."

After he had reclined on a couch and we had sat down on some leather wingback chairs, Holmes recounted the events of the past two days, dwelling a great deal on how the tricks were carried out, in an obvious attempt to put the poor man's mind at ease. But when he had finished, it was clear Dawes still remained unconvinced.

"I tell you, Holmes, this man has power. Perhaps he utilises more conventional stage trickery to achieve an effect, but what about Maddox? Curry? The bloody thunderstorm? No, we must find a way to return the runes to Abcdarius. If we cannot do that, I am finished," he said and began shaking.

"Very well. You are my client, and I have promised to help you. If you are not convinced that this is nonsense, I shall take your burden upon myself. Here is the slip with the runes. Please take it in hand and then place the curse on me."

"That is quite noble of you, but I do believe in this threat and refuse to put you in danger."

"Oh, I do not intend to hang onto them. I should like to see if Abcdarius believes as strongly as you."

"You mean to pass them along to *him*?" I asked.

"Yes, I do, after a fashion."

"Very well. I hope you know what you're doing."

"Let us presume so," said Holmes, holding out his hand.

"Then I place you under the curse," said Dawes with a sigh and handed Holmes the slip of paper.

"And I accept. Excellent. I will return the Tuesday after next at the latest to prove the curse is meaningless. If I bring the business to a conclusion before then, I shall let you know."

After we had returned to Baker Street, we sat down once again, and I asked Holmes about his plans.

"Since you now have the runes, which we know can't actually harm you, isn't that enough?"

"Not at all. Abcdarius could try another ploy to get at Dawes, and I would be disappointed if he didn't turn to me, as well. Keep in mind this is also an opportunity to stop another blackmailer and extortionist before he has a chance to really get started. Finally, I really do want to see the result of my experiment and find out if Abcdarius really does believe. It could prove instructive in later cases."

The bell downstairs rang, and there was a short commotion at the front door. Soon the familiar tread of Mrs Hudson could be heard upon the steps. We both stood to let her in, and she handed an envelope to Holmes that she said had been delivered by a bobby on behalf of Scotland Yard.

"I don't suppose this bobby had a round face and a goatee?" asked Holmes.

"No, he had a hard face with a pug nose, kind of like a boxer's…or one of your informants."

"Morten, the butler of Lufford Hall. Amateurs. Thank you, Mrs Hudson for the package and your opinions," he said rapidly closing the door behind her as she turned to leave.

"He walked over to the mantel, retrieved the jack-knife that was currently impaling his correspondence there, and used it to open the envelope. He withdrew a fluttering slip of paper with some now familiar runes drawn upon it.

"Speak of the Devil," I remarked.

"There's a card, too," he said, handing it to me.

"It's Abcdarius' business card," I read, turning it over. "'Two days are permitted."

"Oh, this is most gratifying and will save so much time," he said, chuckling as he thrust the knife back into the mantel. "I think you can take the day off tomorrow, Watson. I have some business that will take up the better part of the day, and it would be more appropriate for me to attend to it on my own. But please make sure you're free on Friday evening. You'll no doubt want to be present to find out if these old runes actually work, especially now that I am twice cursed!"

So I arranged with Holmes to return to Baker Street on Friday night after dinner and departed for home. I spent the following days catching up with my practice and looking forward to what promised to be a very exciting night. At dinner on Friday evening, I could not stop talking to Juliet about what had already transpired and how completely bizarre the case had been. When it came time to leave, I promised to be careful and not bring home any spirits, malign or otherwise, with me. I did not draw attention to the service revolver I had thrust into my coat pocket. Back in Baker Street, there was no evidence that Holmes had also eaten, but there was a fresh pot of coffee and a dense haze of tobacco smoke waiting for me. The sitting room was almost as cloudy as the sky had been outside. After I opened one of the windows to let in some fresh, if humid, air, we both helped ourselves to some coffee and sat down.

"I had an interesting day yesterday," said Holmes as he lighted his oily clay pipe. He was clad in his mouse coloured dressing gown and slippers, and showed no sign of concern over what would happen at Lufford Hall that evening.

"I thought I would visit Silas Johns and get the measure of him. He and his wife live in Mayfair and are, as Dawes said, obviously quite well off. He was actually engaged upon an errand when I arrived, but one of the servants said he would return soon and was kind enough to let me wait in the library. I could tell the majority of the books were his, as they were the same sort of rubbish we saw in Dawes' study. There was a rare edition of Verhoeven's *On Atavism* that caught my eye, and it was this I was perusing as he entered. I complimented him on it and handed it back as I introduced myself. He was genial enough when I mentioned my interest in the Esoteric Society in the Roseate Morn, but when I said I was most keen to hear more about the Bornless Ritual and if his wife approved of such things, he erupted. Understandably, the man accused me of being in league with Abcdarius, and for a moment, I thought I might have to resort to violence to restrain him. From his remarks, it became clear that Abcdarius is blackmailing him.

"I then told him who I really am and that I am representing Harris Dawes. I talked some more about the other man's plight, as he calmed down. I asked him if he was a true believer and if he thought he saw something that night when they were performing the summoning. He said that, honestly, he had been questioning what he really saw. Denied both food and drink for days before the ritual and having consumed significant quantities of various drugs during it has made his memory uncertain, and he expressed disbelief that he did not notice the camera and its operator behind one of the screens that had been placed around the room. He now acknowledges that it had to have been all about getting the compromising photographs. That is Abcdarius' real power over him. Johns has been paying him to keep the photographs away from his wife, who despite what Dawes' thinks, is the real source of his wealth.

"I offered to assist him, as well, and now have a second client on my hands. He is to meet us at Lufford Hall just before midnight. After that was arranged, I went in search of Wiggins and the rest of the Irregulars. I asked them to report to the Hall today, and they have been duly posted around it. If Abcdarius should leave for any reason, we'll be the first to know."

After that, he settled back and became quiet. I knew better than to interrupt his thoughts. We had been friends long enough that there was no discomfort in the silence. At ten o'clock, he sprang up from the chair and announced it was time to prepare. Soon after, we hailed a cab and were once again bound for Hampstead. The sky was overcast and a great wind had begun to bear down on us, blowing old papers and other detritus about our cab that clipped steadily onward through the city's shadows. When we reached the old pile on the edge of the Heath, we got out of the cab, and Holmes waved to a young boy barely visible behind the trunk of a larch. The lad waved back and disappeared into the night. We then approached the entrance, and Holmes rang the bell. After repeating this two more times, he opened the heavy, creaking door and walked inside. Rain had begun to patter down. The pug-nosed Morten appeared and began to bear down on us from one side of the hall. I placed my hand in my coat pocket, but just then, Abcdarius emerged from the parlour.

"Mr Holmes and Dr Watson! What a surprise this is," he said, checking his pocket watch and holding out a hand for the butler to stop.

"There's no need to be rude, old fellow. Please go back about your business."

He motioned for us to follow him back into the parlour, and as we entered, we apologised to his "mother" for not having removed our hats and coats. They had been playing rummy, and as she looked up at us, Abcdarius looked nervously at his watch again and made a motion with his head. Two enormous thunder claps followed.

"I am so sorry, but Mother and I were just getting ready to turn in for the evening. Mother?" he said, turning to the kindly looking old woman who stood and looked out the window as the lightning flashed. She looked back at Abcdarius, and then muttered under her breath, "Cherry ripe! He's going off."

The magician cleared his throat and resumed after she had left the room.

"Unless, of course, you and Dawes have reconsidered your positions. Please say so, for there is little time left, and you must depart here before midnight."

Dawes was visibly nervous, and we all remained standing. Rain began to pelt the windows and a flash of lightning brightened the room accompanied by an enormous boom.

"No, I am still far from convinced your curses carry any weight whatsoever and am now in a position to prove it. And I do mean 'curses' for I had Dawes place his upon me, as well as the one you so ham-handedly delivered. Speaking of which, how did your seance go the other evening? From your expression I take it all was not well. Pity. As I was saying, your curses don't interest me. Still, I do feel a need to restate my views on magic to you after what I said the other day. You see, I've been thinking it over, and I *do* believe in a certain magic that pervades our natural world. I believe in the power of music and the way it can capture the imagination and change one's mood. I'm certain that sort of magic lies behind all of the arts. I believe in the kind of magic that allows Watson here to sit down with a notebook and pen and summon into existence a story that had never been recorded before. I am amazed by the sort of magic that will allow someone to meet us upon those pages long after we are both so much dust. If we are so honoured that future readers do pick up these tales, will they know that we were real, or will the tales themselves become the reality? That is a real mystery. Yes, I'll take Watson's magic over yours."

"This is, er, all very interesting, but I take it you're not here to deliver a philosophical disquisition," Dawes interjected, starting to visibly perspire.

"Yes, I digress. I asked Dawes to deliberately pass the curse on to me so that I could forward it along in turn."

"Ah, but you couldn't have! I've been watching out for that since your visit the other day. I haven't left the Hall," shrilled Dawes, nervously glancing at the window as thunder punctuated the statement.

"I assumed as much. That's why I passed both his and my strip of paper along to your former confederate, Mr Johns, instead. I believe that's his carriage I hear in the drive," said Holmes smiling. The stomp of hooves and wheels churning up muddy gravel had become audible above the din of the storm. "Abracadabra. It's all just misdirection after all, is it not?"

"No! You don't know what you're doing! If you passed your curse onto him, he cannot be in here with us!" yelled Abcdarius frantically as we heard the front door swing open. "Can't you see, man, we're all in danger!" he shouted, shakily raising his watch to check it again. It was five minutes to midnight according to a grandfather clock in the corner.

The wind was now a steady roar, and a tree limb blew up against one of the windows.

"The demon, it's coming!" shrieked Dawes and abruptly turned and ran out of the room. In the hall, he collided with a startled Johns and caromed into a pedestal, knocking a bust of Asclepius to the floor. He quickly raised himself back up from his knees, steadied himself, and darted out the front door to the astonishment of the pug-nosed butler who was just re-entering the hall.

"After him, Watson!" yelled Holmes sprinting toward the front door. "Johns! Keep the butler and the mother here and out of the way," he ordered as he briefly stopped and thrust a revolver into the confused man's hand.

We ran out into the storm. It was hard to keep Abcdarius in sight with the wind whipping the large rain droplets into our eyes. He had entered a large copse of madly swaying beeches, and despite his lead, Holmes bore relentlessly down on him. I followed from behind as best as I could manage, soaked to the skin. A flash of lightning gave me a brief glimpse of Abcdarius' silhouette about forty yards distant. Then there was a cry, another flash, a large boom, and the silhouette was gone. I came upon Holmes looking down into a small ditch where the magician lay, his head at an impossible angle.

"His foot slipped on that large root there," said the detective, pointing. He then tried to recover his balance by placing his weight on his left foot, but it couldn't hold him, and he fell right over. I'm afraid we'll have to leave him here for the police."

Holmes took off his dripping coat and draped it over the body.

When we returned to the Hall, Johns had both the mother and Morten under cover in the parlour.

"Thank you, Johns. You two, Abcdarius is dead, I am completely soaked, and my patience has run out. Cooperate with me, and I may be able to help you. Act stubbornly, and I will crush you. Where are the pictures and other incriminating materials?"

"Mother" meekly led us to the magician's study and retrieved everything from a safe behind a garish painting of a king draped all in yellow on one of the walls. Holmes left the safe open, but retrieved one envelope, which he handed unopened to Johns when we reentered the parlour.

"The Yard will have questions, Mr Johns, but you have committed no crime. I'll make sure you can rely on their discretion."

The hall was equipped with a telephone, which Holmes used to call in Scotland Yard. I approached him after he had rung off and before he could rejoin Johns and the others.

"Holmes, thank you for all those kind things you said about my work."

"What? Oh, yes. I needed to say something to stall Abcdarius until Johns arrived. Please don't mention it," was his reply.

Holmes did confess to Johns about the runes he had planted in that copy of *On Atavism*, but it was obvious the man no longer really believed in magic, with a 'k' or otherwise. Still, he did return the strips to Holmes to keep as a memento of the case. Dawes, on the other hand, never could be convinced that Abcdarius' demise did not have something to do with that curse. To the best of my knowledge, the Esoteric Society of the Rosiate Morn continues to meet on a regular basis.

The Adventure of the Second Round

It is with much reserve that I begin this account of the mystery which awaited my friend Sherlock Holmes and me at Sherrinsthorpe Manor in Kensington. In fact, not since recording the tragedy of the Cushing sisters have I felt such misgivings about publishing one of Holmes' cases, and in that instance, my reticence did finally prevent the story's inclusion in most subsequent anthologies. Still, the masterful way in which Holmes illuminated such an obscure conspiracy demands no less than that a record be published. Only this and the fact that the passage of time has swept away many of this drama's principal actors have moved me to finally set it down.

It was late in the month of November, and though no snow had yet fallen, the frigid blasts of winter rattled every pane and resonated in every chimney in London. During one particularly bitter morning, I arose shortly before dawn and was surprised to find my friend awake and already dressed. What was even more surprising was that, in spite of the early hour and the forbidding, slate-gray frigidity which had permeated the city, Holmes was in remarkably high spirits. He was standing in front of a roaring fire and filling his morning pipe which comprised all the plugs and dottles left from his smokes of the day before, all carefully dried and collected on the corner of the mantelpiece. Upon my entrance, he picked up a letter which was also on the mantelpiece and turned to greet me.

"Good morning, Watson. I am so glad you've already dressed."

"Good morning to you, as well, Holmes, but I must say that I'm surprised to see you up and dressed so early."

"I was awakened about an hour ago by a messenger," he said, as he handed me the letter. "Do you remember my mentioning an Inspector Nicholson of the Yard?"

"Yes. He has called you in on a couple of cases within the past year, hasn't he?"

"Actually, he has enlisted my help on no less than three occasions. He's very young but has already made quite a name for himself in the press. He was the one who finally managed to apprehend the Spotts gang and that without my help. This time, however, he hasn't wasted an instant in contacting me which can only mean that he has stumbled upon something unusual."

At a nod toward the letter from Holmes, I unfolded it and, in my customary fashion, read it aloud:

"Sherrinsthorpe, Kensington
"3:30 a.m.

"My dear Mr Holmes, I should be very glad of your immediate assistance in what promises to be a most remarkable case. It is something quite in your line. So far, I have been able to keep everything as I have found it, but I beg you not to lose an instant, as it is difficult to leave Lord Morris there.

"Yours faithfully, Geoffrey Nicholson."

"Well, this leaves little doubt as to the result of the crime," I remarked, "but I must confess that the name of the victim is unfamiliar to me."

"It is to me, as well. Since Mrs Hudson has been kind enough to prepare breakfast, why don't you have something to eat while I look him up."

As I sat down to breakfast at the table, Holmes retrieved a red-covered volume from one of the shelves and slumped down into his armchair. When, after several minutes, he stopped flipping through the pages and re-lit his pipe, I hazarded the question: "Well, what does it say?"

"That the victim was noble . . . not that I doubted it. No, I am afraid we shall have to begin our investigation at the scene of the crime."

With that, I hurriedly finished Mrs Hudson's excellent breakfast, and in no time, we had abandoned the comfort of Baker Street for a west-bound cab. Holmes, obviously excited over the prospect of an interesting case, talked animatedly of music and the theatre, but I, uncharacteristically, became withdrawn once our growler entered High Street and the precincts of my old neighbourhood. Even Hyde Park and the Gardens looked lifeless on this relentlessly cold morning, and none but the hardiest tradesmen were out and about. Within an hour, we passed through a wrought iron gate and into a long drive, at the end of which stood Sherrinsthorpe Manor, a massive red-brick mansion of three floors. As we alighted and Holmes paid the driver, a moon-faced and somewhat dishevelled young man emerged from the entrance, said a couple of words to a constable posted by the door, and hurriedly walked over to us.

"Mr Holmes, I'm so glad you decided to accept my invitation!" he said smiling.

"It is good to see you, as well, Nicholson. This is my friend and colleague, Dr Watson."

"It's good to finally meet you, sir. I hate to rush you both, but we should probably have a look at the scene before the coroner arrives to examine the body."

"That's fine, but let me first congratulate you on the birth of your child," said Holmes, causing Nicholson to suddenly turn around again.

"Thank you. Our son Adam was born a few weeks ago. Did Inspector Lestrade tell you?" asked Nicholson with a hint of expectation in his tone.

"No, there are several other indicators. In fact, when I first noticed the wrinkled condition of your suit and that you looked unusually weary, even for one aroused so early, I began to worry that your domestic fortunes had suffered a decline. However, once you turned, exposing the dried milk stain upon your left shoulder, I was glad to find that quite the opposite was true."

"Let's hope Mr Holmes can make such short work of this murder, Dr Watson. Follow me, gentlemen."

And with that, we entered the main hall.

"You will probably want to keep your coats on," warned Nicholson. "As I stated in the letter, nothing has been touched, and the French doors of the study have been open all night."

Indeed, it was absolutely freezing in Lord Morris' study, and I was able to feel a blast of wind the moment Nicholson opened its door which was on the left-hand side of the hall. The French doors were directly across from the entrance, and the only other window, which was closed, was on our left and looked out upon the grounds in front of the mansion. Despite its rifled appearance, the room was neatly furnished, with some scattered Persian rugs, a few armchairs before the fireplace, and a large mahogany desk interposed between the entrance and the French doors. And it was here that Lord Morris sat with his head resting upon the desk's bloodstained blotter. Also upon the desk lay a small pistol, directly in front of his right hand. The man's hunched but tall form still retained its frock-coat with only a pair of black, patent leather slippers indicating that his day's exertions were coming to an end.

"Does that gun belong to Lord Morris, Inspector?"

"Yes, according to the butler, Mr Holmes. It appears to be unfired."

Holmes leaned over and glanced into the gun's barrel. Then, with a nod from Nicholson, he picked it up and began to examine it.

"It is a .41 calibre rimfire, single-shot, Colt derringer. How closely did you examine it, Nicholson?"

"Again, Mr Holmes, I refrained from picking it up, knowing that you would want to see the room exactly as it was."

"That and the wind would account for the error, for it has, in fact, been fired recently. It is obviously a second round which is undischarged," he said, handing the gun to Nicholson.

"Yes, you're right. I can smell the powder."

"What do you make of the wound, Watson?"

I looked down upon a middle-aged profile that had once been quite dashing but was now pale and expressionless and replied, "It is obvious from the burns around its rim that it had to have been inflicted at very close range. In all honesty, Holmes, I would probably have taken this for a suicide, if it weren't for the gun's being loaded. Lord Morris' death would have been instantaneous. The wound seems consistent with this pistol, but until the bullet is retrieved from the skull, it is impossible to say for sure that it is the murder weapon. I assume there is no need to infer the time of death?"

"No," said Nicholson. "Perkins, the butler, heard the shot at approximately 12:45 a.m. and entered the room moments after."

"He saw no intruder?"

"No, Mr Holmes."

"What about all of these papers lying about? Is there anything of any significance?" asked Holmes, as he stooped to look at them.

"Quite possibly there is something significant which is missing, but those I have seen are nothing but household bills."

"Yes. Here is one for coal, for gas, the green grocer's."

"Holmes! There's an appointment book under this armchair," I cried. "It appears the pages corresponding to the past four days have been torn out."

"Excellent, Watson! Why don't you and Nicholson examine the rest of it, while I have a look around."

"Good luck, Holmes. The ground is as hard as a rock out there," replied Nicholson.

Actually, I had almost been able to forget the cold while we were busy in our investigations, but now, I was grateful when Holmes, crawling around on all fours behind the desk, finally made his way onto the patio and closed the French doors behind him. While Nicholson and I paged through Lord Morris' appointment book, I would glance up occasionally to see how Holmes progressed in his search, crawling upon the frozen ground outside, in ever-widening semi-circles. When he returned, I could have sworn he had found some clue.

"What did you find, Holmes?" I asked.

"Nothing whatever," he replied with an odd note of triumph in his voice. "How does your research progress?"

"I told you that you wouldn't find anything out there," said Nicholson. "There's very little of interest in here—mostly Parliamentary meetings and lunch dates with his Bagatelle Club companions. It's all rather pedestrian."

"With whom was the last appointment?"

"His wife," I answered, "for their anniversary dinner."

"I see. May I have a look at it, please?"

Holmes flipped through the book for some time without expressing an interest in any of the entries and then handed it back to the inspector.

"Thank you. I think I'm finished with this room for now. Would it be possible for me to interview the rest of the household, Inspector?"

"Certainly. I have already done some preliminary questioning, and it seems that, since only Lady Morris and the butler were in the central part of the house, only they heard a shot. The other servants were asleep in the wings and have been able to add nothing to the account."

"Then it is to Lady Morris and the butler I would speak. Before we go, however, have you been able to determine who benefits directly from the earl's death?"

"Lady Morris has already been kind enough to show me Lord Morris' will, Holmes. She and their only daughter are the two principal heirs, but I would add that, as things stand, these two ladies are already quite well off."

"Excellent work, Nicholson," commented Holmes, as the inspector led us to the sitting room where Lady Morris was waiting. She was an elegant and stately woman, only just beginning to approach middle-age and dressed in a rather simple, black dress. Though she had obviously been crying, she had regained her composure enough to speak and, at Nicholson's request, dispatched her maid in order to fetch Perkins, the butler. After the introductions, Holmes took a seat in the chair opposite the one in which she sat and assumed his most comforting tone.

"Madam, you do us a great kindness in agreeing to speak with us, and I promise I shall be as brief as possible."

"Mr Holmes, I shall answer as many questions as you like, if they should aid you in catching my husband's killer."

"Thank you. Lady Morris, could you please recount the events of last night, omitting nothing, no matter how seemingly insignificant."

"Yes. I had retired early, before my husband had returned from his club, in fact, and awoke to a loud noise. I heard a door open and close in the hall below and began to hurriedly dress myself. Upon lighting the lamp beside the bed, I noticed that the time was approximately 12:45. Within a few minutes, I descended the stairs and saw Perkins stepping out of the room. I could tell from the expression on his face that something was horribly wrong. Perkins' family has been attached to my husband for three generations, and I know him almost as well as I know anyone. He tried to stop me from entering, but I forced my way over the threshold. I saw my lifeless husband slumped over his desk and immediately fainted. After summoning the maid to take care of me, Perkins called the police from the telephone in the hall."

"Lady Morris, are you positive that you heard only one shot?" asked Holmes.

"A loud noise woke me up, and I heard Perkins enter the study. If there were any sounds before those, I slept through them."

"How long an interval had passed between your waking and your descending the stairs?"

"I did not look at the clock again, but it could have been no more than two minutes."

"Did you notice anything about the state of the room when you entered it?"

"I noticed several papers lying upon the floor and that the French doors behind my husband's desk were wide open."

"The derringer in the study, did it belong to your husband?"

"Yes. My husband was never fond of hunting. It was the only gun in the house."

"Which club did your husband attend that evening?"

"The only club he ever attended: the Bagatelle Club, in Regent Street. He loved both cards and billiards."

"You have a daughter?"

"Yes, she is married to an American railroad owner and lives in San Francisco. She is pregnant with our first grandchild."

"With your permission, Lady Morris, I would like to ask you some more general questions. Can you think of anyone who would want to kill your husband?"

"My husband's affairs were largely his own, but no, I can think of no one. There was, however, someone unknown to me."

"Pray, continue," Holmes said, as he leaned forward, steepling the tips of his fingers.

"Three days ago, on Wednesday evening, I was passing my husband's study on my way to the stairs, and I heard him speaking with another man. I could not make out what was being said, but my husband was definitely talking to someone whose voice I had never heard before. I thought this odd, as no visitor had called upon us, so I entered the dining room beside the study and kept watch at the window, waiting for the stranger to appear. I assumed he had entered the study through the French doors, since he hadn't rung at the front door. I was confirmed in this a few minutes later when a tall man, wearing a black overcoat and a broad-brimmed hat, emerged onto the patio. I had never seen him before, but he was about your height, with a full beard and a slight limp. I am sorry that I cannot tell you more, but it was too dark.

"After that meeting, my husband was a changed man. He did not come to bed that night or any succeeding night, for that matter. I couldn't get more than a few words out of him at a time, and once, when I looked in upon him in his study, he looked as though he had been weeping. The only excuse he would give was that he was concerned over a friend of his at the club, Sampson, I believe, who was gravely ill. This was all he offered, and most of the time, I could barely make eye-contact with him."

"I am sorry," said Holmes. "I have only one more question. Do you remember at what time you came across your husband's meeting with this stranger?"

"Yes, it was almost 9:30 when he left."

"Thank you, Lady Morris. I shall let you know as soon as I have any information."

"Thank you, Mr Holmes and Dr Watson," said Lady Morris, as she and her maid left the room. "Please let me know if I can provide you with anything further."

As soon as she departed, the butler entered the sitting-room. He was slim and in his fifties, with long and graying sideburns.

"Hello, Perkins. I am Mr Sherlock Holmes and this is Dr Watson. I have just a few questions for you."

"I shall try my best to answer them, sir," replied the butler.

"What were you doing when you heard the shot?"

"I was at the other end of the hall, making sure all of the candles and lamps had been extinguished when I heard it."

"You heard only one shot?"

"Yes, sir, and I hurried to the study as quickly as I could. I was sure the sound had come from there."

"At what time had Lord Morris come home that evening?"

"Around midnight, sir. He went directly to his study without saying a word."

"At what time did you hear the shot?"

"When I passed the grandfather clock in the hall, it was 12:45."

"When you entered the study, you found it just as it is now?"

"Yes, sir."

"You saw no intruder?"

"None, sir, but I was slow to act, on account of the shock. It took me a moment to walk over to the French doors."

"Perkins, why did you close the door behind you when you entered Lord Morris' study?"

"I didn't, Mr Holmes. The wind blew it shut."

"Thank you, Perkins. That will be all for now."

Perkins opened the door for us, and our trio re-entered the hall. Holmes turned once more to Perkins and asked, "Would it be possible for you to call Dr Watson and I a cab, please."

However, Lady Morris immediately appeared at the banister and called down, "Nonsense, our driver shall convey you to your lodgings. Perkins, please get Boggis."

After thanking Lady Morris, Holmes, Inspector Nicholson, and I discussed the case outside, while waiting for the coach.

"What do you make of it, Holmes? Was Lord Morris shot with his own gun?"

"So it would appear, Watson. You will telegraph, Inspector, when you know for certain?"

"Of course."

"Holmes, why would the killer load a second round into the gun?" I asked.

"It is much too soon to speculate. Perhaps the killer didn't," said Holmes, with the faintest trace of a grin forming upon his face.

"Nonsense, who else would have done it?" shot back, Nicholson. "It could be that the murderer was trying to make it appear as though a different gun had been used, in order to deflect suspicion from someone within the household. After all, only someone familiar with the house could have found the gun."

"There is a germ of a sound theory in that statement, Inspector. The gun and the room's appearance are definitely meant to deflect suspicion."

"I take it you are referring to the room's being rifled?" I asked.

"Yes, Watson. It is suggestive."

"How so, Holmes?" asked Nicholson.

"An intruder could have had but a minute in which to work, before Perkins entered."

"That affirms my theory that it was an inside job—the killer knew where to find the papers he wanted," Nicholson interjected.

"In any event," I ventured, "I think suspicion rests squarely upon this man in the broad-brimmed hat. Find him, and you'll find your killer."

"Yes, Watson. Once we have this stranger's identity, we shall have solved this case."

"Well Holmes, if you have no objections, after I consult with the coroner, I am going to start questioning some of the people in this address book."

"Very good, Nicholson. Watson and I will visit the Bagatelle Club. I'll contact you, if anything develops."

By this time, Boggis had already arrived with the coach. Before Holmes had given him directions, he asked my friend if he was Mr Sherlock Holmes. Once Holmes had affirmed this, Boggis began to draw closer and speak confidentially.

"Mr Holmes, sir, there is something that has been troubling me about the master, but I'm not sure if it's something I should mention to the mistress."

"Go on, Boggis."

"You see, sir, I'm the one what always drives his lordship to the club, and sometimes, his lordship asks me to pick up some of his friends, as well. Lately, not Lord Morris, but a couple of these friends have been mentioning something peculiar, a 'Bagatelle Shakespeare Society'. But they always sound real smarmy when they say it, like lechers in a dancehall. Now I'm no better than any other bloke, but it seems to me that these two friends had some kind of corrupting influence on his lordship. Does any of this help you, Mr Holmes?"

"Yes, Boggis. Tell me, had you ever driven Lord Morris and these friends to any destination other than the Bagatelle Club?"

"No, sir. Just heard 'em talk is all."

"Thank you, Boggis."

Holmes said hardly a word on our drive back to Baker Street. I knew better than to interrupt my friend during such spells of silence, for he would undoubtedly reveal all at the appropriate time. Our trip was, therefore, rather monotonous, except for a quick stop at the post office, so Holmes could send a telegram. When we finally arrived at 221B, Holmes tipped Boggis most generously, and we ascended to our rooms, Holmes to await a response to his telegram and I to await the lunch which Mrs Hudson was preparing. After I had eaten, Holmes having elected to instead consume a heroic amount of shag for lunch, I sat down in my armchair and rested my legs upon an ottoman heaped with cushions, for the cold had been bothering my old wound terribly. It was just after I had finally gotten comfortable when two telegrams arrived for Holmes.

"Ah, the first one is from Inspector Nicholson, confirming that Lord Morris' derringer did, indeed, fire the fatal shot. The second is from the Earl of Maynooth."

"The father of Ronald Adair? Is he back in England?"

"He has been back for some time, Watson, and has agreed to meet with us, at the Bagatelle Club. Perhaps he will be able to shed some light upon the affairs of Lord Morris."

Once again, we hailed a four-wheeler and were soon on our way to Regent Street. It was still quite gloomy and cold, but at least the wind had finally died, making our trip somewhat more comfortable. As we approached our destination, I felt a wave of nostalgia as I gazed upon the white façade of the Criterion Bar, for it was there that I first heard mention of Holmes, an event which changed dramatically the trajectory of my life. There was little time for reminiscing, though, for we had soon reached our destination. Upon entering the club, a small, elderly man in the most neatly pressed suit I had ever seen began leading us past table upon table of cigar chewing nobility, all enjoying their games and their brandy.

"Once again, we are moving in high life, Watson," quipped Holmes with a sly smile.

We then arrived at a comfortable, oak-panelled alcove where sat an ample-framed, florid-faced gentleman whom I took to be the Earl of Maynooth.

"Hello, Mr Holmes. And Dr Watson, it is so good to finally meet you. Too bad about Lord Morris; terrible business that. I shall do what I can to help, but I must admit that I did not know the man terribly well. Please, take a seat," he said, indicating two sumptuous leather armchairs. After Holmes and I had accepted and lit the cigars our host had offered to us, Holmes addressed the earl.

"I realise, sir, that you were not close to Lord Morris, but was it his custom to stay here until late in the evening?"

"Why Mr Holmes, I, myself, no longer keep very late hours, so I could not positively answer your question."

"Lady Morris said her husband spent a great deal of his time here, but another source of mine intimated that he may have been here less frequently than she thought. Would you, by any chance, know anything about that?"

"Lord knows I have enough trouble keeping track of my own affairs and could not possibly be expected to keep tabs on a veritable stranger. I do know, however, that the earl and a few of his friends were rather fond of the ladies, Mr Holmes."

"Yes, that is the very thing about which I need to know more."

"I am afraid I do not know much more than that. Besides, it is not fitting for a man of my position to engage in such cheap gossip."

"I understand, sir, but I am afraid that, to find out what happened to the late earl, I must press the issue. What was the Bagatelle Shakespeare Society?"

"Not so loud, man. And do not think for a moment that I would ever forget the service you and Dr Watson performed for my family in risking both of your own lives to apprehend my son's murderer. I would not miss any opportunity to help you, but I must be discreet. Lord Morris and two of his friends, whose names I will provide to you should it become absolutely necessary, liked to prowl the theatres of the West End in search of conquests. The practice started when the earl met an actress at the Burbage Theatre by the name of Cecilia Benson. He was quite fond of her and went to see her regularly. She then introduced some of her friends to Lord Morris' companions. Since all of the men are married, they would usually come here first and then depart for the Burbage later in the evening."

"Thank you, sir. You have been a tremendous help. Tell me, before we go, how is Sampson getting on?"

"I'm afraid I know of no one by that name. Is he a member?"

"Evidently not. Sorry, my mistake. Come, Watson. We must get to the theatre before it opens for the evening. Hopefully, we'll have time for a word with Miss Benson."

"*Mrs* Benson, Mr Holmes," the earl corrected. "Cecilia Benson is married, as well."

A short time later, Holmes and I, after another silent cab ride, found ourselves in the Strand before the Burbage Theatre. According to the signs out front, Cecilia Benson was appearing as Volumnia in *Coriolanus*. We made our way through the large, richly carpeted lobby, the walls of which were lined with caryatides of gilded plaster, to the manager's office. At our knock, a small, rather high-strung man emerged, and we introduced ourselves.

"It is a pleasure meeting you, Mr Holmes. To what do I owe the honour?"

"It is imperative that I speak to one of your actresses, a Mrs Cecilia Benson."

"Indeed, I too would like to speak with her, for you see, she's been missing for the last four days."

"Holmes, that corresponds with the missing pages of the appointment book!" I said.

"You wouldn't happen to know who saw her last?" queried Holmes.

"Well, sir, that would probably be me. On Tuesday afternoon, I was gazing out of my window at a strange carriage I had noticed which was parked in front of the theatre. Within moments of my turning to look outside, I saw Cecilia walking towards the carriage with a man. They climbed inside, and off they went. I've been making do with her understudy, ever since."

"Could you describe the man who accompanied her?"

"I didn't get a good look at his face, but he was quite tall and walked with a pronounced limp."

"Was he wearing a broad-brimmed hat?"

"Why yes, Dr Watson. He was."

"What was it about the carriage that struck you as odd?" Holmes resumed.

"It was the insignia upon the side, a cross, in front of which was something resembling a fluttering sheet of linen. Over this, were the initials 'St V'."

"Holmes, there was a man named St Vincent listed in the appointment book!"

"Thank you, Watson. Sir, would it be possible to see Mrs Benson's dressing room? It might help me to find her whereabouts."

"Certainly, Mr Holmes. Follow me."

The dressing room was fairly small, its large dressing table taking up most of the space. Amongst the make-up and brushes littering this was a small notebook which Holmes immediately began to examine.

"Watson, there is a page missing."

Holmes then produced a charcoal stick from his pocket and began lightly rubbing the right-hand page which would have lain beneath the missing one. In this way, he was able to reveal the following faint message:

"My Darling,

"I am to be admitted this afternoon. Please come."

Holmes then searched the rest of the tiny room but revealed nothing further. Finally, we took our leave, Holmes promising to contact the theatre manager, if he found the missing actress. Before returning to Baker Street, Holmes dropped into a post office to send two telegrams. In the cab, on our way home, I could remain patient no longer.

"Homes, what can it all mean?"

"Surely, Watson, a man of your background should have no problem finding our fugitive actress' location."

"All I can make of it is that she is to gain admittance somewhere with someone who might possibly be named St Vincent."

"Come now, Watson. The note says nothing of 'gaining admittance' but of being 'admitted'. Surely, that would suggest something to someone such as yourself."

"Well, in my profession, one is usually 'admitted' to a hospital."

"Precisely. Now, let's assume that 'St V' does not stand for the name of an individual."

"I'm sorry, Holmes, but I don't follow."

"The cross, the linen, 'St V', surely that would indicate St Veronica."

"St Veronica's Hospital for Women! Of course."

"Yes, Watson. I have just sent a telegram to them, asking if Mrs Benson is a patient and if we can pay a visit tomorrow morning."

"To whom did you send the second telegram?"

"To our good friend, Nicholson, apprising him of our progress."

It was already dark when we arrived back in Baker Street, and I was relieved when Holmes decided to join me for dinner. That night, I fell asleep to the melancholy strains of Holmes' violin and did not re-awake until some time after dawn. When I entered our sitting room, Mrs Hudson was already setting our breakfast upon the table, and Holmes was reading the paper.

"Good morning, Watson. Have a seat. There should be ample time for breakfast before we resume our investigation."

"You certainly are in a good mood, Holmes."

"I have just heard from a Dr Smythe, at St Veronica's. Mrs Benson is, indeed, a patient there, and we are free to visit her at any time after eleven o'clock. I expect this meeting will go a long way in establishing a motive for our case."

"Does that mean you know who killed Lord Morris?"

"My dear Watson, I have known that since yesterday morning."

"But who?"

"All in good time. I must satisfy myself upon a few more points, before I can be absolutely certain of events. Would you like to have a look at today's paper? It contains an account of what we saw yesterday at Sherrinsthorpe."

After breakfast, we departed for the East End. It was there, in the City, that we found the rather ugly pile of a structure known as St Veronica's Hospital for Women. It was, in reality, more of a mental asylum than a traditional hospital, and its sterile, white, arched corridors reverberated with the screams and moans of its imprisoned Bedlamites. Dr Smythe, a rather shabby looking bald man with a flaming orange beard, was leading us through a throng of black and white uniformed nurses to the room of Cecilia Benson.

"Here we are, gentlemen, but I must warn you that my patient may not be of much help to you," he said as he swung open the room's heavy door.

Even with no make-up and dressed in a shabby white hospital gown, Cecilia Benson was a stunningly beautiful woman. Her flawless, milk-white skin was emphasised by her long, black hair, and her movements were still incredibly graceful, reflecting her several years upon the stage. Yet, when I looked at her eyes, I noticed a vacancy in their gaze, and I could also detect a slight slackness about the mouth.

"Oh, Smythe, you have brought me company, and a handsome pair they are," she said, touching Holmes' arm.

He did not attempt to hide his distaste and quickly brushed it away. "Mrs Benson, I would like to ask you some questions about Lord Morris."

"He is dead and gone; at his head a grass green turf, at his heels a stone," she rambled.

"I take it, then, that you know what has happened. Do you have any idea why?"

"As if he had been loosed out of hell to speak of horrors, he comes before me," she said as she turned to me and placed her hand on my leg. Like Holmes, I deflected it but, admittedly, with a greater reluctance.

"Mrs Benson," resumed Holmes, "can you tell me anything of your husband?"

"I was the more deceived," she said sadly. "There's fennel for you, and columbine; there's a rue for you; and here's some for me."

"O, what a noble mind is here o'erthrown," said Holmes in frustration while turning to leave.

"You are a good chorus, my lord," replied Mrs Benson, and as we left, she began to sing:

"For to see mad Tom of Bedlam
"Ten thousand miles I travelled

166

"Mad Maudlin goes on dirty toes

"To save her shoes from gravel."

Once outside the door, I made my diagnosis, "Dr Smythe, it appears Mrs Benson is suffering from syphilis."

"That is correct, Dr Watson. She admitted herself on Tuesday and has very rapidly deteriorated."

"You say she admitted herself? There was no one with her?"

"No, Mr Holmes. She mentioned that her physician had referred her to us but, upon questioning, could not seem to recall his name."

"Thank you for all of your help, Dr Smythe."

While we were walking back to our cab, Holmes began to speak.

"Watson, we must have the name of that doctor."

"The one who gave the referral."

"Yes, if you could call it that. Would it be possible for you to find out the identity of Lord Morris' physician?"

"I imagine I could make a quick stop over at Bart's and see if any of my colleagues know anything."

"Excellent, Watson. We shall drop you off there, first. I have some business to attend to back in the West End. Remember, get as much information as possible, and meet me back in Baker Street, before supper."

As we agreed, late that afternoon, I returned triumphantly to Baker Street. Holmes was already seated in his armchair with his feet propped-up on the fender before the fireplace.

"Good afternoon, Watson. How did you fare?"

"Holmes, Lord Morris' doctor's name is Edmund Samuels. He has offices in Wimpole Street and was in a riding accident two years ago, causing him to walk with a pronounced limp! Here is his address."

"Brilliant, Watson! You have outdone yourself!"

"It is just as you have said, Holmes: 'When a doctor does go wrong, he is the first of criminals. He has nerve and he has knowledge.' It now looks to me like this is all simply a failed attempt at blackmail. But Holmes, where are you going?"

"I have to send one more telegram, Watson. I expect developments. Go ahead and have supper without me. There is no need to wait on my account."

Indeed, Holmes ate nothing that night and shunned sleep, as well. The next morning, I perceived him dimly through a fog of tobacco smoke. He was smoking impatiently, obviously awaiting a reply to the telegram he had sent the previous evening. It arrived shortly after breakfast.

"Watson, I must leave to notify Nicholson and Lady Morris that we shall meet them at Sherrinsthorpe Manor this afternoon. It is at that time that I will clear up this matter for them. You will accompany me, I presume."

"I wouldn't miss it for the world. But really, Holmes, you must eat something."

My entreaty fell on deaf ears, however, and I was left to finish my breakfast in solitude. Later, that afternoon, Holmes, Inspector Nicholson, Lady Morris, Perkins, and I once again found ourselves in the sitting room of Sherrinsthorpe Manor, and everyone but Holmes took a seat.

"Mr Holmes, am I to understand that you have, in fact, solved this case?" asked the inspector.

"There are but two points which I need to clarify. The first and most pressing of which is how you managed to procure the second derringer round so soon after discovering the body, Perkins."

The butler practically leaped out of his chair and exclaimed, "Surely, Mr Holmes, you don't think I killed Lord Morris?"

"Nothing of the sort, Perkins, and please, resume your seat. Why don't I reconstruct the events of the evening, as I believe they occurred, and you can fill in the gaps for me when I have finished.

"After you heard the shot, it could have taken you no more than forty-five seconds to reach the room. This event could not have been totally unexpected by you, and you will also have to explain to me how you knew what had driven Lord Morris to suicide. It is obvious to me, however, that you did know, because you managed to rearrange the room so quickly, obscuring what had really happened. You entered the room and closed the door behind you, for if the wind had been strong enough to blow that door shut, it would have also created a larger mess within than what was there when we examined it. Somehow, you found a second round for the gun, and with that came your idea. You reloaded the weapon and replaced it, wiping the powder marks from the earl's hand. To minimise the chance of anyone noticing the odour of the discharged weapon, you opened the French doors which also made it look as though an imaginary intruder had used them. From the appointment book, you quickly removed the pages which would have scandalised Lord Morris, and it was this which prompted you to create the illusion of the room's being rifled by the imaginary killer. After scattering a few papers from that cabinet, you reopened the door and waited for Lady Morris to appear which would have been moments later. Am I correct so far?"

Perkins nodded in bewilderment, while Lady Morris sobbed.

"But, Perkins, why?" she cried.

"Madam, Perkins was acting out of a misguided sense of loyalty. However, I am afraid I must point out that Lord Morris' present behaviour deserved no such fidelity or respect. In truth, Lady Morris, he has used you horribly. Of late, Lord Morris had become romantically involved with an actress. Unfortunately, as I found out yesterday, she, too, had been the victim of a husband with a roving eye, and from him, she had contracted a *morbus veneris*. She, in turn, passed this disease on to your husband who, unable to cope with the shame, decided to take his own life."

"He's right, Lady Morris. I came upon the earl, weeping in his study on Thursday. He tried to compose himself and mentioned an ailing friend, but when I observed the doctor's bill upon his desk, he broke down and confessed everything to me. Essentially, he and I grew up together, and I suppose, at that moment, he had to confide in someone. It was also at that time that I noticed the derringer in a drawer of his desk. I had never seen it before, so naturally, I thought the worst. Later that evening, I returned to the study and removed the bullet from the breech of the gun, putting it in a pocket of my frock-coat. I knew it wasn't my place to do so, but I hoped that, if Lord Morris knew that I had figured out his intention, somehow, it might deter him. The following night, when I heard the shot, I knew immediately what had happened. As I walked down the hall, I reached into my pocket for a key to the study, in case it should have been necessary, and I found the bullet. The rest is as Mr Holmes said, though I have no idea how he could have known it. Please, Lady Morris, you must understand that I was simply trying to protect Lord Morris."

"At great risk to the health of Lady Morris," chided Holmes.

"Holmes, how did you know it was a suicide?" asked the inspector.

"As Dr Watson said, the posture of the body and the wound were all consistent with suicide. Why would a killer want to make a crime scene which looks exactly like a suicide look like that of a murder? Also, there was no sign of an intruder. As I said before, how could the butler come into the room within one minute of the shot's being fired and not have discovered the killer going through the appointment book or the cabinets? There really weren't terribly many papers lying about on the floor, but to a butler, it would seem like this degree of dishevelment was consistent with a robbery of some sort. No, Nicholson, only the body seemed to be undisturbed. All else seemed rearranged, and there was only one person we knew of who would have had the opportunity to alter the room's appearance. Given all this, all I had to do was discover the reason for the suicide. This proved more time-consuming than I had anticipated."

"What about the man in the broad-brimmed hat?"

"That, Nicholson, was Lord Morris' physician, Dr Edmund Samuels. According to this telegram I received today, he had come here on Wednesday to examine Lord Morris. He has promised to contact you, as well, Lady Morris, tomorrow."

"Well, I suppose I must now decide how to proceed in the matter."

"Inspector Nicholson, as you and several of your colleagues have already learned, your career can only benefit from working with me from time to time and by placing the utmost trust in my conclusions. However, just because *I*, who am in no way connected with the official police, have come to this particular conclusion does not mean that you, *Inspector*, are in any way officially obliged to accept or act upon it."

"Thank you, Mr Holmes. I shall take that under consideration."

Privileging honour over self-advancement, Nicholson never did officially solve the murder of Lord Morris, a momentary setback in a career which would soon be redeemed by many successes. At that moment, however, Holmes and I were still unsure of the outcome. It was already growing dark as we made our way home, and outside our cab, a wind had begun to blow from the east, and the snow had finally begun to fall.

The Adventure of the Earl's Mirth

It had been an unusually busy December for Sherlock Holmes with the great detective shepherding no less than three cases to successful conclusions. Though his endurance throughout that flurry of activity never flagged, after it concluded with his stunning testimony at the sensational trial of Hoffman, the counterfeit cheesemonger, I could detect significant signs of strain upon his customarily indefatigable and restless nature and had thought to offer him an excuse to recover over the holidays. A few days prior to Christmas, a patient I had recently been seeing presented a perfect opportunity, if only I could persuade Holmes to agree to it. When I returned to our rooms at 221B Baker Street, I tried my luck.

"You know, Holmes, since we took up rooms here, you have introduced me to a great many fascinating and downright colourful individuals. I feel, in a spirit of giving appropriate to the season, that I should do my best to return the favour," I said over my shoulder from my desk. Holmes looked up at me curiously as he continued to fill his pipe.

"A couple of months ago, I began seeing a patient, who I thought might interest you, but of course, due to patient privacy, I couldn't readily mention. The other day, however, he put those concerns to rest. Do remember that last performance of the Philharmonic we attended at St James Hall? You remarked upon the ability of the cellist."

"Nathaniel Harland. Yes, Brahms first cello sonata. His fingering was extraordinary," replied Holmes, closing his eyes and pausing for a moment to remember the piece. "Are you saying he is your patient? Out with it, man."

"Indeed he is. There's a minor but stubborn issue with his wrist from hours of daily practice that I've been treating. Stubborn as it has been, though, I have been able to help, and he has offered in return to host the two of us at his ancestral estate in Sussex for the holidays. I've mentioned you to him a few times, and he would very much like to meet you. He emphasised that you must bring your violin and be prepared to play."

"My dear Watson," said Holmes, "I appreciate the offer and the concern that prompts it, but you must understand that, though many look forward to escaping the dark, chill days of winter by celebrating and basking in the warmth of family and friends, the criminal classes are not always among them. Given the unusually fecund start to the month, it would be remiss of me to quit London now."

"But Holmes, it is only West Sussex. Surely if some criminous Scrooge delivers his masterstroke while we are away, we shall get word of it and be able to return to London in no time. And as a doctor, I can tell that you are fatigued and not functioning at your full capacity. Why, you have been sitting at your desk for hours staring down at the monograph you've been working on for days and scarcely writing a word"

"An admirable deduction, Watson, but as usual, an erroneous one. To be perfectly honest, I am beginning to wonder if a second volume on the variability of human ears may be excessive, if not downright self-indulgent. And besides, I would surely have got further along last night if it weren't for Mrs Hudson's continual interruptions. Honestly, have you ever seen this much holly and ivy in one place? There is scarcely a surface left bare. And your efforts with that tree…," he complained, gesticulating to the small tree Mrs Hudson and I had installed and decorated in a corner of the sitting room.

"But Holmes," I persisted undiscouraged, "Think again of St James Hall. How can you pass up such an opportunity? The man promised me that he will be at your disposal to discuss and play."

His gray eyes softened.

"You're right, of course. It is an honour, Watson. You have certainly been fortunate in your friends. I shall clear up some small matters and be ready to depart on whatever day you and Lord Harland arrange. After all, if there is an emergency, it is not as though it takes any time at all to get to London from West Sussex."

It was in the early afternoon of December twenty-third when Holmes and I boarded a train at Paddington Station bound for West Sussex. The platform was full of excited and cheerful holiday travellers, both arriving and returning, many of which were carrying packages wrapped in colourful paper. As we boarded, a Salvation Army band began to play "God bless Ye, Merry Gentlemen".

"Truly a magical time of year, is it not, Holmes?"

"That it is, Watson, and I must admit that I am looking forward to our holiday."

We had arranged for a private car, and after settling in, Holmes talked animatedly about the various Philharmonic concerts we had attended and what made them distinctive. As we made our way south, the first snow began falling gently upon the rolling landscape with London's environs gradually giving way to the countryside and, eventually, the South Downs. Within a few hours, we reached the station where Lord Harland, himself, awaited us on the platform as we alighted.

"Welcome, Watson. And you must be Mr Sherlock Holmes. I am so glad you both could join us for the holidays."

"The pleasure is all mine, Lord Harland. I was just regaling Watson with the details of some of your, and your colleagues', performances."

"You flatter me, sir. We shall have to play this evening, Mr Holmes, if you would like. Come, my groom will help you carry your bags to my carriage."

We left the station and loaded our belongings and ourselves onto the carriage. After a short drive through the chilly, whitening Downs, we passed through the tiny village of Stepworth, the nearest to Harland's estate, and Harland pointed out various local landmarks, many constructed in the Sixteenth and Seventeenth Centuries. Having passed through the quaint town, we soon approached a large metal gate bearing Harling's family crest and two large Christmas wreaths. A smiling caretaker emerged from a small nearby cottage to unlock the gate for us and wave us in. We then proceeded along a long drive that ended in a semicircle before a large gray stone pile of a mansion with many gables and mullioned windows. As we approached the large, wreathed front doors, they were thrown open by a young man in a frock coat.

"Thank you, Jones. This is Mr Sherlock Holmes and Dr John Watson. Jones is a new addition to the staff, the youngest butler I can ever remember serving at Harland Manor. He will lead you to your rooms."

There was a fire roaring beneath a holly and ivy strewn marble mantel along one wall of the enormous hall and, just beyond it, the largest Christmas tree I have ever seen, decorated in a host of blazing lights and tinsel. More holly, ivy, and yew adorned the oak bannisters of the richly carpeted stairs on the opposite wall, and we followed the butler upstairs to our rooms. These, too, were cavernous and furnished with four-poster beds. More ivy and wreaths adorned the mantels and the walls in these chambers, as well. It was all like something out of a fairy tale.

For the next couple of hours, Holmes and I unpacked and refreshed ourselves before joining Harland for dinner. His brother and niece were in London while his brother attended to some business, but Harland assured us they would return before supper tomorrow. After an exquisite dinner, we retired to the drawing room to smoke our cigars and pipes. The panelled room was filled with sumptuous leather armchairs, a circular oak table with a chessboard inlaid upon its surface, and another large and brightly decorated Christmas tree with several brightly wrapped presents lying beneath it. Inhaling the fresh scent of the spruce, I hunkered down by the roaring fire and turned my chair toward the French windows on the far wall so that I could drowsily watch the snow fall. Harland and Holmes sat a few feet away and within a few minutes, had begun to play. For the next couple of hours they played a repertoire of pieces that, though they sounded familiar to me, I had not the knowledge to identify. I sat smoking and drowsily admired the interplay of the two instruments, violin and cello, weaving in and around each other as the snow fell outside. Eventually, they both fell silent.

"I hope you do not mind my mentioning it, but there appears to be a picture missing from above the mantelpiece, Harland," observed Holmes. "Another wreath, perhaps?" he asked while tucking his Stradivarius back in its case.

"I must confess that is my household's own little mystery. It was a painting called 'The Earl's Mirth'. A portrait of the old Earl Harland, like the one out in the hall but by a different artist. I came into the room last Monday morning, and it had vanished without trace. There's a bit of a legend about it if you are interested."

"Extremely, do go on," said Holmes, puffing at his briar-root pipe while his keen gray eyes sparkled. I could not suppress a smile at his instinctive reaction to a potential puzzle.

"The old Earl Harland was a notorious Elizabethan recusant, though he was never suspected as to have gone so far as to throw in with Spain. He did have to flee England and somehow managed to save his fortune from confiscation, if not his property. Later, the family, having reevaluated their religious views, reappeared, were allowed to return to their lands, and, once again, managed to thrive, but the original fortune was never recovered. We always joked that it could still be buried in Ireland or somewhere.

"Legend has it that, as long as the missing portrait remained in the house, the Earl would someday emerge from it and restore the family's fortune. Not that our family did badly without him. No one ever took it seriously, but the painting has always been a sentimental favourite, a sort of family reminder that all reversals of fortune are fleeting and should be met with pluck and optimism, I suppose.

"You know, another funny thing about that portrait.... You see, it is very unlike the one that hangs in the hall," said Harland, looking off into the distance. I had noticed the other painting earlier. It was a very lifelike rendering of a corpulent, bearded man in traditional Elizabethan finery. The sort of portrait you would expect to see of a Sixteenth Century nobleman.

"This one was very crudely done, very amateurish. But I have often wondered if it didn't capture the nature of its subject more accurately. In it, my ancestor is depicted as laughing uproariously. It is, from what I know about portraiture of the period, a very idiosyncratic pose. My niece, who is only ten with the vivid imagination of a child, claims that she has actually heard the old man chuckling. And, about a week before the painting vanished, she said that the Earl even spoke to her. She said he told her that he was soon going to depart to gather his fortune. It was the oddest thing...but I, personally, should very much like to have him back."

"You said it disappeared without trace. Lord Harland, I have some experience with such things, and I can assure you that nothing ever vanishes without a trace. Did you report it stolen?"

"No. I would like it back, but...I really do not want to deal with the hassle and the drama of a police investigation. You see, I have my suspicions as to who might have taken it. My last manservant, the one Jones recently replaced, left under a bit of a cloud. He also had an interest in art, having studied as a painter before entering service. He was engaged to my last cook, but things became stormy. One morning, they had a row that was extremely loud and embarrassing. I had no choice but to let them go. They departed a month and a half ago.

"In any case, I notified several people I know in the art world and auction houses. I am hoping that it will turn up so that I can reclaim it. Please do not trouble yourself over it."

"Oh, but a little mystery could not help but add zest to our little holiday. Would it not, Watson?"

I emitted an audible sigh and lit another cigar.

Holmes rested his chin upon his clasped hands in a characteristic gesture and closed his eyes.

"You said there was no evidence of a break in?"

"No, whoever took it came and left without disturbing anyone or anything within the house."

"And who was in the house on Sunday evening?"

"The servants, of course. My brother and his little girl, Emma. His wife passed during childbirth, and he is raising the girl on his own. He lives in London but has recently been considering moving back to Sussex. I have offered him an entire wing to himself. We have always been close."

"Is there anyone else who is familiar with the legend of the painting who might have taken it seriously?"

"The former butler, Dodson, had asked me about it more than once."

Holmes directed his gaze toward the spot where the painting used to hang and contemplated for a moment with a dreamy expression.

"Was there anything else that was unusual about the painting, Harland? Can you describe it more fully?"

"Well, as I said, the old boy was leaning back laughing. Not in profile but turned slightly. And pointing with both hands," said the Earl, mimicking the pose to unintentionally comic effect.

"Pointing where, exactly?" asked Holmes, leaning forward.

"You know, it was the funniest thing, Holmes. I have remarked more than once as I sat over there playing chess that he always seemed to be pointing at me and my opponent and chuckling at us."

"Funny is precisely the word, sir. What if the 'mirth' referred to in the title indicated not just referring to his mood but also its object?"

"How do you mean, Holmes?" I asked as I stood up and wandered closer.

"This table, Harland," said Holmes, rising and walking over to the circular oak table with the chessboard. "It looks like it is actually joined to the floor. Is it not?"

"Yes, it is original to the Manor and could not be moved without effort. That has always been perfectly fine by my family, since it would be hard to imagine it in any better location."

Holmes then got down on all fours and began examining the base of the table and the floor with his glass. After a few minutes, he sprang up abruptly and grabbed hold of both sides of the table, his lean, athletic frame exerting a great deal of force to get it to turn very like a large ship's wheel. To our surprise, it slowly did and we heard a loud click along the wall to the left of the entrance. As we turned to look, a piece of the panelling along the lower part of the wall swung out into the room, revealing a space behind it. After we walked over to investigate, Holmes retrieved a lamp from an end table and held it within the opening. We saw that it was a stone stairwell leading downward. On the opposite wall of this strange portal, facing us, lay a small wooden box in an alcove. Holmes reached in, pulled it out, and opened it. Inside was a small piece of parchment on which could still be read:

> "Out of the pit
> "Ascend the heights
> "Your reflected gaze
> "Beyond the fragile army
> "The broken teeth
> "The shard of glass
> "A spinning wheel"

"What on earth could it mean, Holmes?" I asked.

"I could only guess at this point. Let's see where this staircase leads first, shall we."

He stooped and crawled into the entrance and then descended the stairs with us following close behind.

"Note these broken cobwebs. Someone has passed through here recently."

After descending about fifteen feet, we came upon a straight narrow passage and began to follow it. Holmes stopped a few times to examine the dust upon the floor.

"Yes, I believe we have found how the person who took the painting gained access to the house. It is getting colder."

"And we are surely no longer under the house," observed Harland.

"The light at the end," said Holmes pointing. Within a few more minutes we emerged at the base of a small hill, like the entrance to a small mine. The house stood about two hundred yards behind us.

"This is remarkable. How could this entrance have escaped our notice for all these years?"

"I imagine it was well concealed until recently. Allow me to take a quick look around, and then we can return."

The detective walked about, examining the ground, but it was clear that the snow was frustrating his efforts. After a few minutes, we once again entered that strange passage to the house. Coming back into the drawing room, Harland and I sat by the fireplace. Holmes, however, remained standing, his lean frame propped against the mantelpiece while he examined the parchment he had once again retrieved from the crude wooden box.

"I should like to hang onto this and study it, if I may, Harland."

"Of course, but what do you think it all means?"

"It is too soon for me to speculate. I must have more data," he said before pocketing the parchment and producing his pipe from his pocket.

"Where is the post office in Stepworth?"

"It is just around the corner from the Hart and Hare, the village inn. I am sure you noticed the sign as we drove through town."

"I recall the inn, but I remember the sign was missing."

"Was it? I didn't even notice. They have been doing some renovating lately, so I suppose it is not surprising."

At that point, I could no longer stifle a yawn.

"Ah, but it has been a long and unexpectedly exciting day, has it not, Watson? Now it is getting late, and I think it is time we retired for the evening."

After breakfast the next morning, Holmes left me to catch up with Harland with instructions to keep a look out for any new developments. He rode into Stepworth with Harland's groom to do some exploring while the servant conducted some errands prior to the evening's Christmas Eve dinner. The snow had stopped the night before, and Lord Harland's brother, the Honourable Sir Robert Harland, arrived on time with his niece in the late afternoon. He was more sturdily built than his brother, with darker hair and a walrus-like moustache. His daughter, Emma, in contrast, had very light hair and the typical shyness of a child. Lord Harland's groom returned shortly after their arrival but without Holmes, who he said had been detained in the village but promised to return in time for the evening's dinner. Since everyone soon became very busy with Christmas preparations, I retired to my room to read for a while before getting dressed for dinner.

When we did sit down at the table in the long dining room, Holmes still had not returned, but Lord Harland was in a festive mood and barely took any notice. The snow had begun to fall again, and in the candlelit glow of that holly encircled room, looking at all of the steaming silver platters before us, it would have been difficult not to feel the joy of the season. And, yet, I could not help but notice that something seemed to be bothering Sir Robert. More than once, our host had to repeat a question to him, because he was distracted. And even I, who had never met the man before, could tell he was unusually tense.

Holmes arrived at the same time as the soup and had managed to dress and join us in no time.

"You know Robert, Holmes, Watson, and I discovered the most extraordinary thing in the drawing room last night after we had been playing our instruments. I was only waiting for Mr Holmes to return to tell you all about it."

I was surprised to see the colour visibly drain from Sir Robert's face, and could tell that Holmes, with his keen sense of observation, had noted it, as well. Lord Harland, Holmes, and I then began to recount the events of the night before. In contrast to Sir Robert's inexplicable apprehension, the smiling Emma seemed to delight in the story.

"I do wonder what happened to that picture. Do you have any ideas yet, Holmes?"

"I do, and I am afraid that, by confirming them, I have ruined a little surprise that was planned for this evening's festivities. Sir Robert?"

Sir Robert, exhaled loudly and took Holmes' words as a cue.

"I am truly sorry for any concern I have caused you, Nathaniel. It was all meant to be a surprise. You see, I am the one who took the painting."

"But why on earth would you do such a thing, Robert?" said Lord Harland, flushing.

"To have it copied, so that it could replace the old sign of the Hart and Hare, which Sir Robert has recently purchased."

"Why, Mr Holmes, that is exactly what I did. I was going to return with the original this evening and surprise you all with the painting and the news. Purchasing the pub last month was one of my motivations for returning to Stepworth. I was going to mention it to you when I was visiting shortly after the deal was made, but you were out that evening playing bridge. Emma and I were in the drawing room, recounting the old legend, when she noticed that the old boy seemed to be laughing at the table with the chessboard. The same idea then struck me that struck Holmes last night. I could not believe I had not noticed it before. After I walked to the end of the passage, the idea to make the whole thing a surprise for Christmas came to me. I did have to clear the mouth of the outside entrance, but I was able to quickly manage that with a shovel the next evening without anyone seeing me. Emma and I concocted the story about the Earl talking to her, which she delivered to you with the skill of an actress, and I made off with the painting that Sunday night. I took it to a local craftsman in Stepworth who has painted most of the signs in the village so that he could copy it, but…"

At this point, Sir Robert paled again and began to visibly tremble.

"But it was not there when I went to pick it up today. Someone else, pretending to be my agent, had already claimed it."

"Before I utterly ruin your Christmas Eve dinner, Sir Robert, as Watson has probably already guessed, that person was me," said Holmes, his gray eyes twinkling.

"I had planned last night to go to Stepworth today to send a few telegrams regarding the missing portrait, but some things your brother said last night had struck a chord with me. First, he had mentioned that you intended to return to Stepworth. Next, there was the story about your daughter saying the painting had spoken to her. Then, when he was giving me directions, he mentioned the sign of the Hart & Hare, which I had noticed was missing. He also mentioned that it was being renovated. I had been turning these facts and others over in mind. Before going to the post office to pursue other inquiries, I stopped in to chat with the innkeeper, and it was then that I heard about your purchase, Sir Robert. I walked around the village until I saw a recently painted wooden sign hanging in front of the tearoom, and I asked them who had painted it. That led me to your craftsman, Alvin Woodcock. Please do not blame him, though. A very young man was behind a desk in the shop when I entered, obviously an apprentice, and he was the only one there. I told him I was your employee and asked him if the sign was ready. I then waited until dark to sneak back in through the passage to restore the painting to its proper place before making a more conventional entrance at the front door. I do not know if you noticed, Warson, but there was a lever to the right of the door of the secret entrance so that it could be opened from the opposite side.

Once again, I apologise for causing you any concern, Sir Robert. Please let us continue with this magnificent meal and you can tell us more about your plans."

As we continued to dine on the plentiful quantities of goose, roast beef, and puddings before us, Sir Robert, much relieved and reinvigorated, told us about how he had always admired the old inn and that it formed part of a plan for him to become more involved in the daily life of the village when he returned to the Manor. After dinner, we all withdrew to the drawing room, as we did on the previous night, and there we saw the old Earl, beaming and laughing at us from above the mantelpiece.

"There is something for you, Sir Robert, beneath the tree just there," said Holmes.

Sir Robert smiled and walked over to retrieve a brightly wrapped package from among the others lying beneath the glowing tree. His smile widened as he unwrapped the object and proudly held it up for us to see.

"This turned out even better than I had hoped. Behold, the inn's new sign!"

On the square, a wooden sign was an excellent likeness of the chuckling old Earl with the inn's new name emblazoned beneath: "The Earl's Mirth".

"What a delightful way to spend the holiday season," proclaimed Lord Harlan, "with a genuine mystery solved by a real detective. Thank you, Sherlock Holmes."

"But Holmes," I could not help cutting in, "I believe there is still another mystery. What about that strange parchment? Have you worked out the meaning of it."

"I believe I have, Watson, but let's ration ourselves and save that for tomorrow morning after breakfast, for there are still drinks to be had and ghost stories to tell."

Christmas morning dawned, crisp and cold, and we accompanied our host and his family to the morning service at the chapel in Stepworth. We then returned to Harland Manor, and as we got out of the carriage, Holmes returned to the subject of the riddle of the parchment.

"I propose we go for a walk before Christmas dinner and see if we cannot make something of this little puzzle that has been left for us."

Everyone was still extremely curious about it and was dressed for a walk in the snow, so we followed the lithe form of Sherlock Holmes, garbed in his travelling-cloak and ear-flapped cap, as he set off briskly across the grounds toward the low hill where the secret passage terminated. As we walked past the large and ancient pines, oaks, and beeches, the wind began to pick up, and was accompanied by snow flurries. Fortunately, only a few inches lay on the ground and did not impede us. When we reached the entrance to the secret tunnel, Holmes stopped and furrowed his brows.

"I believe this to correspond to the first line, 'Out of the pit.' Here, Watson," he said, handing me the parchment. "What is the next line?"

"'Ascend the heights.'"

"And the tallest hill is over there, just to the north," he said, before heading out to the spot. Upon ascending to the top of the hill, we looked out over the grounds of Harland Manor, our breath producing small clouds in the cold air.

"A commanding view of the estate, eh, Watson?" asked Holmes as he surveyed the landscape, like a bird of prey.

"What is the next line?"

"'Your reflected gaze.'"

Holmes surveyed the scene around him, closed his eyes, and contemplated for a minute.

"Was there ever a pond on the estate that would be visible from this spot, Harland?" he asked our host.

"Oh, good show. Yes, ages ago, before I was born. Even with the snow, if you look closely, you can just make out an indentation over to the east. It was quite small. There is another larger one over that hill there, but I cannot see it from here."

"Then let us proceed."

Once again, Holmes marched off toward the next destination, and we trooped excitedly behind. Arriving at the spot where the pond used to be, we continued with our bizarre Christmas ritual.

"This one's even more abstract–'Beyond the fragile army.'"

Holmes furrowed his brow in thought for a moment.

"And what is beyond 'the fragile army'? I'm sorry, Watson...the line after that?"

"'The broken teeth.'"

Holmes made a clicking noise with his tongue and began marching.

"Does that copse of bare beeches over there not resemble a rag-tag bunch on the march, Watson? And look, just beyond– those large protruding stones."

There were, indeed, a group of six very jagged stones protruding from the ground to the south, whether arranged by ancient man or nature, it was impossible to tell. Within a few moments we were among them. A few were even taller than Holmes.

"I believe we are almost at our final destination, are we not?

"Yes, Holmes. There are only two more lines: 'The shard of glass' and 'The spinning wheel.'"

"A 'shard of glass' and a 'spinning wheel'," he muttered as he paced among the stones.

"Does this stone not look almost semicircular?"

I looked at the stone which was, more accurately speaking, oblong and protruded about five feet out of the ground.

"If I squint."

"Come, Watson, Christmas treasure hunting is serious work," he said smiling. He began to examine the stone more closely as we approached. "Aha, there it is–a distinctive smooth spot. Much smoother than the surrounding surface and almost certainly polished by human hands. Perhaps the same trick twice," he said as he grasped the stone and began pushing it, as though he were trying to roll it away from him. It did not budge. He repeated this from the other direction but still produced no result.

As he stood by the stone, wrinkling his brow and chewing one of his nails, Emma approached him and said quietly but matter-of-factly, "Mr Holmes, doesn't a spinning wheel have a pedal?"

Holmes looked at the girl, grinned, and then startled her by dropping on all fours and brushing the snow away from around the base of the rock. He made a sudden exclamation and stood back up, brushing the snow off his clothes.

"And there is the pedal, Emma," he declared, putting his foot down on a small square stone that was parallel to the large one, which he once again began to push away from himself. And it rolled. Rather, it shifted forward, revealing a four foot square hole in the ground, containing a battered iron chest. Dropping to his knees and lifting the chest from the ground, he sat it down beside him, produced some tools from his coat, and began working at the lock.

"Perhaps the fortune is real after all, brother," said Lord Harland grinning with the same excitement and exhilaration we were all now feeling as we gathered more closely around the kneeling Holmes. Within minutes he had sprung open the box, which was, disappointingly, practically empty. There was another small piece of parchment, which made him laugh out loud when he read it. He then gathered three stray coins from the corner of the box, polished them on his cloak, and handed them to a fascinated Emma.

"Three antique gold sovereigns, our Christmas treasure," he said beaming at the young girl who was obviously thrilled with the find.

"And a note from the old Earl, I believe," he said, handing me the piece of parchment.

"'No Treasure lies here to behold, you Dastard.

"'O'er Channel fled it to enrich this B...'

"Well, let's just leave it at that. Colourful chap, your ancestor."

"But judging by those final feet, not much of a poet," said Holmes.

"It does confirm what the family has always suspected about his fortune," said Lord Harland.

"And his character." added his brother, chuckling

"Indeed, the clues were evidently a rather elaborate joke at my expense. Still, I cannot think of a better way to spend Christmas Day or remember a more enjoyable holiday. I am indebted to you for inviting us, Lord Harland."

"I wholeheartedly agree, Mr Holmes, and I doubt Emma will ever forget it," said Sir Robert.

"Ah, yes, I do have one more thing for you, Emma," said Holmes, producing a shilling from his coat.

"There is an army of young people in London who often assist me with my cases whom I call the Baker Street Irregulars. Without your help today, I would not have been able to solve the riddle of the parchment. I am also greatly impressed with your apparent acting ability. It would be an honour for me if you would accept this shilling and join the ranks of the Irregulars."

Emma took the proffered coin, and threw her arms around the great detective.

"Excellent. Treasure hunting is hungry work, is it not? I believe, if we head back to the Manor now, we should just have time to clean and warm ourselves up before dinner."

Cheerfully, we set out once more toward the welcoming warmth of Harland Manor, singing carols all the way.

About the Author

Mark Wardecker first met Sherlock Holmes and Dr Watson in a Golden Press collection of stories that was included with two other volumes in a slipcased edition of mystery and horror fiction purchased at an elementary school book fair. Sadistically, the editor of that collection decided to conclude it with "The Final Problem", but the resulting childhood trauma that caused was soon remedied by a trip to the library where his mother checked out *The Return of...* and other volumes of Holmes adventures for him. A couple of years later, he began watching the Granada series on PBS with his father and became completely hooked. He has been a devoted fan ever since, and has contributed pastiches (most of which are contained here) to *Sherlock Holmes Mystery Magazine* and *The MX Book of New Sherlock Holmes Stories* and an article to the *Baker Street Journal*. He is also a devotee of August Derleth's Solar Pons pastiches and is a member of the Praed Street Irregulars (invested as "The Missing Tenants"). He has even written a couple of Pons stories himself for *The New Adventures of Solar Pons* (which resemble two of the stories included here if you squint) and is the editor of *The Dragnet Solar Pons, et al.* Aside from the Sherlockian material, he has contributed a variety of fiction and nonfiction to other publications. He lives in Maine and is an instructional technologist at Colby College.

CPSIA information can be obtained
at www.ICGtesting.com
Printed in the USA
BVHW031522121122
651757BV00018B/712

9 781804 240533